"Who did you say you might be, stranger?"

MacKail put down his beer and said, "I'd be Stringer MacKail from the *Frisco Sun*. I hope you'll notice I'm reaching for my wallet with my left hand."

Watson nodded and Stringer got out his press pass and I.D. to show them as he said, "I was sent up here to do a feature on the Great Yana Uprising. I hope it's not a private fight."

"We thought we'd about won, until this afternoon," Watson said. "Young Saunders here brung his fellow deputies in full of arrows. We told 'em to let sleeping dogs lie. But did they listen?"

Saunders seemed more interested in Stringer than in Indians as he hovered his gun hand near his tied-down Colt '74 with a heap of thoughts running around in his sly gray eyes. He waited until Stringer was putting his wallet away before he went for his gun . . .

LOU CAMERON

STRINGER

AND THE LOST TRIBE

CHARTER BOOKS, NEW YORK

STRINGER AND THE LOST TRIBE

A Charter Book/published by arrangement with
the author

PRINTING HISTORY
Charter edition/December 1988

ISBN: 1-55773-120-9

Charter Books are published by The Berkley Publishing Group,
200 Madison Avenue, New York, New York 10016.
The name "CHARTER" and the "C" logo are trademarks
belonging to Charter Communications, Inc.

PRINTED IN THE UNITED STATES OF AMERICA

10 9 8 7 6 5 4 3 2 1

CHAPTER
ONE

Grandmother Hitaga felt sure she could go no further. The sharp teeth of more than fifty winters had gnawed the strength from her bones, and the saltu bullet in her back did nothing to make her feel any stronger.

High above, her star sisters danced in the same familiar way, but nightfall had caught up with her amid hills her band had not walked before, and this was frightening, frightening, for who could say the names of the people, or ghosts, who lived this far from the Valley of Many-Colored Rocks?

The Mechi-Kuhi said it was a good thing to find a nice place to sit down and sing your death chant when you were feeling too weak to go on living. For should the spirits find a body simply sprawled among the ferns, they might mistake it for a dead animal and not gather its ghost at all. It felt bad enough to be lost in the dark as a person; she didn't want to be lost in these strange surroundings as a ghost. But still she staggered on through the oak and chaparral, even as she wondered, dully, why she still seemed to be on her feet.

Then, as she rested a moment against the friendly smoothness of a madrone sapling, she knew. For the night breeze was bringing her the sound of distant drumming. It had to be a spirit drum she was hearing. It had been a long time since real people had dared to make so much noise among these hills. But she had no other place to go that wasn't dark and empty. So she let go of the sapling with a word of thanks for its help and staggered in that direction, thinking that at least she would save the Death Spirit the trouble of looking for the place she fell.

Many painful steps later, Grandmother Hitaga could hear the voice of the drummer as well. His words were good to hear. They were in her own language, and the spirit sang with the voice of a man, chanting over and over again: for a thing that was good to hear should be sung many times, and only a restless spirit might ask why a singer didn't stop saying he was going to hunt a lot of deer and just go do so.

Grandmother Hitaga pressed onward until she saw the glow of a small fire through the trees. It looked warm, and now that the sun stayed up a shorter time each day, the mountain nights were getting colder. The weary, wounded woman could not think of the dangers lurking near so many night fires. She was ready to die now, as long as she could warm up a little before her big sleep.

And so, a few minutes later, as Grandfather Tetna chanted his dream song in the entrance of his bark wowi, something made him glance up from the glowing embers of his fire, and his voice was silenced by the coldness he felt in his throat. For the figure he saw between two trees at the far edges of the firelight did not seem that of a real woman. She was wearing a robe of woven rabbit-fur strips, the kind of clothing his own grandmother had made when he was a boy—the kind of robe no real woman bothered to make anymore. The old man tapped the drum on his knees, and softly called out, "Hear me, Spirit. If you are my grandmother's ghost I welcome you, and if ghosts eat, I have some acorn mush I can heat up for you. But if you are an evil mechi, go away! and don't come back!"

Grandmother Hitaga sobbed. And then she closed her eyes and fell down.

After she had run like a deer for many moons, with the saltu, the mechi, and other bad things chasing her, Grandmother Hitaga opened her eyes again to see she was inside the wowi with the old man, who wore saltu clothing and had one of those saltu grease lamps burning brightly. She lay naked on a pile of itchy saltu blankets, with another thrown over her. Someone had tied a cool wet wad of healing herbs against the bullet wound in her back.

The old man, who must have done this, cleared his throat and said, "The bullet was stopped by your shoulder blade. I did not think I should wait until you woke up for permission to dig it out. You had lost much blood. Your robe was sticky with it, and I am sorry to say I tore some strips getting you out of it. But I have many blankets, and you can have one to wear as soon as you feel better. I have a pot of mush and fresh sticks on the fire out front. I am called Tetna. I used to be a great warrior, but now I am just an old man, as you can see. I camp up here to be alone during the harvest moon. The younger men and even some of the women have gone down to Fat Valley to gather a grass they call barley for the saltu. They are given presents for doing this. I tried it once. I did not like it. The work in the fields was hard enough, but after dark everyone got drunk and fought half the night. It is better up here among my friends the oaks. When the harvest in Fat Valley is over, my grandsons bring me some of the good things the saltu make, anyway."

The wounded woman stared up at him. "Your band is on good terms with the saltu? How is this possible?"

To which the more assimilated Indian could only reply, "I am not sure. But it seems to be so. Long ago we fought them. Most of us were shot down with those bang-sticks, of course, and they hung our Majapah from an oak branch until he died. But then a less cruel saltu told us he was our agent. I am not sure what that means, but it seemed to be a good thing to have. The agent seldom bothers us, and since we have had him the other saltu only call us damned diggers and hit us once in a while. The agent won't let them shoot us with their bang-sticks anymore. But I see someone shot you not long ago. Don't you have an agent?"

Grandmother Hitaga shook her head sadly. "My band has always tried to avoid saltu, good or bad. Like your band, we had trouble with them when they came into our world to search for that yellow dust that settles along so many streambeds. Our wise Majapa led us to the Valley of Many-Colored Rocks, where there has never been any yellow dust. Now and then a saltu did wander through our gathering grounds. But it was easier to hide among the ferns than to fight him until he had dipped his pan here and there or broken off some bits of rock to take away with him and never come back."

Grandfather Tetna nodded in approval. "That was a good way to deal with them. I wish we had thought of it. The saltu can be very cruel when you fight them. But how did you get shot if you were having no big trouble with the sickly pale creatures?"

The old woman sighed. "Trouble came to us just a few moons ago. Many saltu came to our valley to dig for things they valued. There has never been any yellow dust there, but they keep digging anyway. They must have a bad spirit driving them. They dig like moles for a red rock that is only good for making medicine paint. They even dig up the bones of our long-dead and put them in siwinni boxes. They build bigger boxes to live in, even if it is where someone has always dug bulbs or gathered acorns. They are evil. When some of us tried to make them stop spoiling our gathering grounds, the saltu yelled a lot and struck them down. When our young men could take no more of their rudeness there was a big fight."

Grandfather Tetna didn't ask who'd won. He asked cautiously, "Do the women of your band join the men in such matters?"

She shook her head. "We didn't have to. After the bone-stealing saltu beat our young men in battle they went after everyone. I was hiding among the ferns with some other women and many children when some saltu came riding those four-footers of theirs and started shooting at us. I don't know how many of the others got away. I almost got away unharmed. But then, as I ran through the trees, something hard as a rock and hot as fire hit me, and as soon as I feel stronger I must run some more, I think."

The old man hunkered over her and shook his head. "Just lie still. Nobody will shoot at you here. They call the hills around here a reservation. Nobody but us may hunt or gather around here without asking the agent-saltu if he will let them. Hear me. If the agent asks about you I will tell him you are one of us. Maybe I will tell him you are my marimee. Do you think that would distress you?"

Grandmother Hitaga smiled in a way she had not smiled at any man for some time. "Before I make love to any old man, even a good-hearted one, I must do something about those evil saltu and anyone among my old band who may still be alive. I feel sorrow in my heart when I think of strangers digging up my ancestors' bones. I am old. I am only a woman. But I have to do something to those saltu who came to spoil the gathering grounds of my people. You are a man, Tetna. If you really like me as much as you say, you should be thinking of a way to help me."

The old man felt a stirring of pride he had not felt in many a summer. For Hitaga was pretty, even if her hair was a little gray in places. He said, "I have been thinking, ever since I dressed your wound without that blanket over you. It is a bad thing to shoot a woman. Even some saltu say this. I think we should send for my grandson, Joseph. His mother named him that because she follows the medicine of the Jesus Ghost. He has not been brought up in the true way, but he has a good heart."

The wounded woman brightened. "If your grandson knows saltu ways, he might be good at fighting them.

Do you think he will help us drive those crazy saltu from the gathering grounds of my band?"

Grandfather Tetna replied soberly, "Not by himself. The boy is barely a real person, let alone an initiated warrior. But he has saltu friends. Hear me. This is possible, as crazy as it may sound to you. One time my grandson rode with the blue-sleeves in the faraway fight the saltu had with the Spanish band. He often boasts of a saltu friend he made in a place called Cuba when they saved each other's lives in a bad fight they were having. Joseph used to call his saltu friend MacKail. Lately it has been changed to Stringer for medicine reasons, I think. Joseph says his good friend Stringer makes little black medicine marks for all the other saltu to read. I don't know how they do that. But Joseph does, and he says Stringer always makes his little black marks tell the truth."

Grandmother Hitaga looked dubious and muttered, "I did not know any saltu could tell the truth." But the old man hushed her and insisted, "My grandson is not saltu. So he could hardly be lying when he says he would trust Stringer with his life. I think Joseph should go find Stringer for us. If Stringer tells all the other saltu that bad saltu have been digging dead people up and shooting at live women, some agent may read it, and nobody but an agent can drive saltu from the gathering grounds of real people."

Grandmother Hitaga remained dubious. "What if this saltu friend of your grandson refuses to help us? Why should any saltu help us at the risk of his own life? Those crazy ones who shot me are very ferocious, you know."

Grandfather Tetna shrugged. "It is worth a try. Someone has to help us, and my grandson says that in Cuba his friend Stringer was very ferocious too."

And so, less than a week later, Stuart MacKail of the *San Francisco Sun* was typing up a rewrite in his furnished room on Rincon Hill when an almost naked lady walked in on him without bothering to knock. An open kimono was some improvement on her usual state of dishabille. For the gal on the second landing worked nights as an artist's model at the California School of Fine Arts and seemed to feel there was no great reason to change from her work clothes as she lounged about at home.

It seemed almost as rude to go on typing as it did to look at her. So MacKail fixed his eyes on the envelope in her hand as he got politely to his feet and asked if there was something he could do for her.

The Gibson Girl in the open kimono cast a wistful glance at the brass bedstead against the far wall but answered, "The mailman just left this downstairs, special delivery. I know your last name is MacKail. But what kind of a first name might *Stringer* be?"

The man the urgent letter had been sent to held his hand out for it as he explained, "Stringer is my nickname. It's too involved and unfunny to explain to anyone outside the newspaper game. Uh . . . don't you usually leave for work about this time every afternoon?"

As he tore the envelope open she cast another wistful glance at the bed and replied, "I do, damn it. The landlady is out, and none of the other boarders have come home from work yet. But c'est la goddamn vie, as we artistic types say."

He didn't answer. He was scanning the block-lettered message from his old war comrade, Joe Malliwah.

She wafted closer to his bed as she murmured, "I don't think they'd really fire me if I turned up a little late. How do you feel about shutting your door and making sure it's locked?"

He gulped and answered, "I'd be fibbing if I said the thought never crossed my mind, ma'am. But right now I have to get over to my office, pronto, before my feature editor can light out for the weekend. This news tip is too hot to sleep on."

She insisted she had to be at least as hot as any old special delivery letter, damn it. But Stringer had already scooped up his hat and coat and was dashing out the door and down the winding stairs as she flung maledictions about his manhood after him. They were hardly fair, but a man who messed with such tempting stuff where he boarded or worked was asking for more trouble than even a great lay could be worth, even when he didn't have more important matters to attend to. So by the time he'd made it out the front door and swung downslope to the north he had the temptation to turn back under control, and by the time he'd crossed Market Street, dodging trolley cars and horseless carriages, his hard-on had subsided entirely.

The rush-hour foot traffic bucked him all the way to the cast-iron facade of the *Sun,* and he had to bull his way in against the torrent of stenographers and such on their way out of the building. But the *San Francisco Sun* never set, as the old saw went, and so, as he'd hoped, old Sam Barca was working late, as usual, in the little frosted-glass box they kept him in lest he shock female staffers of the newsroom with his pungent Parodi

cigars and muleskinner's comments on the lousy ways
of the new twentieth century. Old Sam had started out
sticking type at a time when they hadn't allowed women
to enter a saloon, board a clipper ship, or—damnit—
work anywhere near a newspaper.

But this evening, as Stringer dragged a bentwood
chair after him into Barca's corner cage, the bald old
bastard actually looked cheerful. He smiled up from behind his cluttered desk. "I was just about to send a
printer's devil to fetch you, MacKail. Have I got a feature assignment for you!"

Stringer swung the chair around to sit down, cowhand style, as he waved the envelope in one hand like a
quirt and replied, "I was just about to say the same
thing. But you go first, Sam."

"It just came over the service wire from up north,"
Barca said. "I can't believe it. I thought we'd seen the
last of such doings at Wounded Knee. But here we are
in a new century and we've got us an Indian war to
cover."

Stringer said dryly, "I'd hardly call Wounded Knee a
war, and might we be talking about some troubles up
near Mount Lassen?"

Barca scowled. "Who told you? It just came in. A
mining outfit operating in hitherto uncharted country
has been trying to keep a lid on the troubles they've
been having with some unreconstructed Digger Indians.
But it's gotten to be more than their company police can
cope with, and now they've asked the Army for the
usual help."

Barca took a thoughtful drag on his evil-smelling
cigar before he added, "Having covered such matters as
the Modoc war in my misspent youth, I imagine most of

the fighting should be over by the time you can get up there. But you ought to be able to get the makings of a nice Sunday feature from the locals up that way. With any luck there ought to be some human-interest obits. So far the Diggers have arrowed at least four mining men and scared the shit out of a lot more."

Stringer took out the makings of a defensive smoke. "Back up, Sam. I was just about to say I wanted to cover the story. But for openers, the Indians we're talking about ain't exactly Diggers, and they tell the story a different way."

He tossed the letter from Joe Malliwah halfway across the desk and began to fill his cigarette paper with Bull Durham as he explained, "Joe Malliwah is an Indian cowhand I met up with in Cuba, during the war with Spain. He was serving with the Rough Riders, and one night, when we came under Spanish sniper fire, I was sure glad he was on our side. He allowed his folk were Yana and that he'd been born on a reservation, but he gave up such notions once he saw how much fun it was to play cowboy instead of Indian. As you'll see when you get around to reading his letter, Joe has some less assimilated kin living higher up in the hills. He's not sure why they want to go on eating acorns and manzanita, either. But Joe says that's all they were doing when some saltu, as they call us, invaded their secluded glen and started to bust things up. Joe allows an arrow or more had been pegged at the mining men, but he insists they started the trouble, and, so far, Joe Malliwah has never lied to me or anyone I know of."

Sam Barca shrugged. "I told you I covered many an Indian war when I was as young and idealistic as you, MacKail. But ours not to reason why, and how many

Indians buy the *San Francisco Sun?* You know I'll let you turn in the truth, and, hell, we'll even run it, if it's a good story. Just don't let the truth get in the way of a good feature. There's no news in a mining camp tough screwing a begging squaw and getting beat up or worse by her buck. I want you to make it sound like the Great Sioux Uprising, even if you have to make up some feathers and pad the casualties a mite. Our readers could use some safe excitement, now that they're surrounded by street lamps and damn fool regulations against wearing guns to town on a Saturday night. If your old Army pal is right and the peacetime Army behaves as dumb as usual, we might just get a stirring account of campaigning in the wilderness after Indians that might not be there. Remember Chief Joseph and Captain Jack?"

Stringer looked pained. "I was still learning to rope and say da-da, if I was around at all. But I recall the legends, and you're right—the peacetime Army can surely cover a heap of ground riding in circles after nobody much. I'd best get up there before the soldiers get too lost to interview."

As he rose, Barca said, "Grab the S.P. line north and get off at Los Molinos. The wagon trace along Mill Creek ought to carry you on up to the scene of the massacres."

"That's where Joe Malliwah said to get off. He'll be waiting with some ponies. After that it gets a mite more complicated. Joe says all the trouble is on the far side of Mount Lassen, in the hills we've never bothered about before."

Adding that he had a few errands to tend to before he caught the night train, Stringer left before his boss could ask just what he had in mind. For Barca had often forbidden him to ever go near the Presidio again. Old Sam just didn't find the military notions of old Teddy Roosevelt as amusing as he did. But Stringer wasn't out to write about chrome-plated bayonets or whitewashed battleships right now, and what Sam didn't know couldn't make him have another raving fit. So Stringer hailed a motor taxi out front and told the driver to haul him around Russian Hill and out to the old Presidio.

West Coast Army headquarters was an open post, so the poor MP's posted at the main gate had to wave them through. Stringer had never figured out why there had to be a round-the-clock guard at a gate the general public was allowed to pass through at will. Mayhaps they'd run out of rocks for the soldiers to paint white. As he got out in front of the officers' club, a father and son were cutting across the parade ground with some fish they'd caught, likely near Fort Point, the brick blockhouse guarding the south entrance of the Golden Gate against any enemy craft smaller than a river gunboat. They'd erected Fort Point during the Civil War, nobody could say exactly why, and thanking God for small favors, it had never been fired upon by the local fishing fleet. Its breakwater was a swell place to fish, though.

He saw they'd been polishing the brass cannon in front of the officers' club again. It was an antique muzzle-loader that had been cast in Spain and taken as a war trophy when Mexico gave up the bay area without a fight. It was sort of pretty, though, with all those baroque curlicues shining in the sunset's orange glow.

Inside, the enlisted barkeep shot a thoughtful look at Stringer's civilian suit and old Army Stetson. To save the confused barkeep from asking, Stringer said, as he bellied up to the bar, "I'm not a member, but I feel sure

my old pal Colonel Lowe must be. Do you reckon I
could have a boilermaker while I wait for him to show
up?"

The soldier behind the bar still looked confused.
Regulations were one thing, and a civilian on drinking
terms with a bird colonel was another. So he said, "I can
serve you the beer part, sir. Each officer's private stock
is stored secure and, well, private."

Stringer allowed that was a sensible way to keep hard
liquor on an Army post and said beer would be fine.
When he'd been served a handsome schooner of suds
and asked how much he owed for the same he was told
there was no charge. He was pleased to learn the taxpayers only had to spring for chasers. But as he was
saying so a voice growled in his ear from behind, "You
know damned well that all the expenses of this club are
paid for from the members' own pockets, MacKail."

So Stringer turned to smile at the lean and hungry-
looking gent with red hair on his head and silver eagles
on his shoulders, saying, "Evening, Colonel Lowe. I
was hoping to find you here, after such a hard day's
work at GHQ."

The somewhat older but well-preserved officer grimaced and replied, "I'm not supposed to grant interviews
to you anymore, MacKail. What ever possessed you to
write that the Krag is a lousy rifle? Ordnance was upset
as hell to see that in your damned old paper."

Stringer shrugged. "I never asked them to send all
the way to Sweden for such a dismal weapon, Colonel.
But that's not why I'm here right now. I'm covering that
Indian trouble up near Mount Lassen, and I thought you
boys might let me tag along."

Lowe ordered his private bourbon out of its locker,

and as the barkeep placed a tumbler in front of him, the gruff but decent enough officer said, "Better break out another glass for this pest, too. I'm about to ruin his evening for him, so he could use a shot."

As his orders were being carried out, Lowe turned back to Stringer. "A short colonel named Roosevelt let you tag along at a place called San Juan Hill, as I recall, and it was really dirty of you to cable that famous charge as it really happened. But, praise the Lord, you won't get to do that to *me*. So bottoms up."

Stringer clinked with the colonel, threw back the bourbon, and chased it down with some beer before he insisted, "President Roosevelt isn't sore at me about that anymore. We got to know one another up in Yellowstone more recently, as we were both chasing buffalo poachers. I have to allow old Teddy's a pretty good hunter, and he said he admired reporters who told the truth—as long as he could get elected, anyway."

Colonel Lowe nodded grudgingly. "I read what you wrote about those poachers being dumb enough to shoot pet buffalo while the President was making a personal inspection of the park. Your story was pretty good. But the reason you can't tag along up north after the Army is that we're not going. We have it on the authority of the Bureau of Indian Affairs that the Yana are an extinct tribe."

Stringer laughed. "That's the first time I've ever heard the Army and the BIA agree on anything. Of course, since you're both paid to think wrong-headed about the vanishing red man, it figures you'd have to come up with the same mistakes now and again. I just got a letter from a paid-up Yana who'd no doubt be surprised to learn he was extinct. My boss just got it on the wire that some whites up north are bitching about Indian attacks and calling on the Army for help. I sure am starting to feel confused this evening."

The colonel refilled both their glasses as he explained, "Some few Indians listed as Lord-knows-what on the BIA rolls may or may not claim some Yana blood. Meanwhile the BIA assures us none of their agents have reported any trouble on any of the reservations up in that corner of the state. We can't mount an expedition against wild Indians every time some infernal Digger begging at the back door upsets some white housewife by letting his old dong hang out."

Stringer asked how come. The colonel sighed. "Because of reporters like you, for openers. Do you recall the so-called Modoc War up that way a few years back?"

Stringer admitted it had been before his time. Lowe said, "I wish I could say the same. I'd just graduated from the Point, and guess where they sent me to fight Indians?"

He indicated a red and blue ribbon on his chest as he went on. "Calling Modoc Diggers would be to flatter them. Lava lizards would be a better description. They were crawling about the lava flats up near the Oregon line, Lord knows why, when their leader, the one we called Captain Jack, took it in his head to dust up some whites who were crowding him and his little band."

Stringer said that sounded fair. The colonel shrugged. "Maybe it was. I wasn't there. I just got to ride with the Army column sent to put down such an awesome uprising."

He bolted more bourbon and repressed a shudder. "I mean, there wasn't a full cavalry troop to the whole damned tribe, and we were chasing what amounted to a small street gang over lava flats they knew like the heads of their own dicks. They fought on foot, if that was what you wanted to call mean kids popping out of lava tubes like rabbits to make faces and peg shots at us at inconvenient times. Captain Jack and his young toughs were a matter for dismounted policemen with billy clubs to deal with. But no, we were expected to make gallant cavalry charges at big war bands. So that's what we did, even though it was hell on our mounts. Horses were just never made to gallop across a jumble of clinkers and busted beer bottles. It was a real pain in the ass, and they say the hills around Mount Lassen are volcanic too."

Stringer nodded, sipped some more beer, and observed, "But you nailed Captain Jack in the end, didn't you?"

Colonel Lowe nodded. "We did, and in the end he was hanged as the common criminal he was. We could have caught Billy the Kid or Jesse James that way, given enough time and military manpower. But the U.S. Army is not a damned sheriff's posse. It looks a lot less foolish fighting real wars with real enemy armies. So we've wired Lassen County that it's up to their own sheriff to deal with mere handfuls of unruly Digger kids."

"What did their sheriff have to say about your helpful suggestion?"

"He claims it's not his fight," the Army man replied. "He agrees with the BIA that if the Yana aren't a long-dead tribe, any left over haven't been bothering anyone who ever voted for him."

Stringer frowned down at his glass and mused, half

to himself, "Joe Malliwah wrote that the mining outfit is new in the area and operating in a remote valley no whites have ever settled near before. So, in other words, it stacks up as a private fight betwixt the company police and some leftover Indians nobody cares all that much about."

The colonel nodded. "It is. And it will be until things heat up enough to worry the outside world. You've no idea how many requests we get to charge at scattered handfuls of reservation strays. We're keeping an eye on some more ominous Paiute at the moment. Their leader, one Shoshone Mike, could even give us some trouble in the future, at the rate he's been stirring things up over in the Great Basin. Wouldn't it be a bitch if we had another serious Indian uprising in the brand-new twentieth century?"

Stringer grimaced. "It sure would. I thought we were supposed to just watch Indians and Wild West outlaws at the nickelodeon, now that things have got so modern. I reckon some old-timers ain't caught up with modern times yet. Kid Curry told me just before he died that he went to see *The Great Train Robbery* before he held up his last train. He spoke English, too. I wonder how long it's going to take Indians to savvy folk ain't supposed to act so un-modern anymore."

He drained the last of his beer schooner, put it down empty with a nod of thanks to all concerned, and said, "I'd best get up yonder to cover them Indian troubles before someone beats me there with a moving picture camera. I'd be fibbing if I said I wasn't glad the Army wasn't interested."

"Oh, we're interested," Lowe said. "We're just not

ready to move unless and until things get out of hand up there."

Stringer nodded. "Well, I'd best go home and pack, then. I owe Joe Malliwah, and he's expecting me to keep things from getting as out of hand as they've already got."

CHAPTER
TWO

There was no sense getting off a train in the dark with nobody waiting for him. So after Stringer had put on his field outfit of blue denim and checked the timetables at the Mission Street depot he wired Joe Malliwah when to expect him in Los Molinos. Then he walked to the ferry building at the foot of Market Street, toting his possibles in a battered gladstone, to board the Oakland ferry. Twentieth century or not, there was just no other way to catch the main line up to Los Molinos unless one enjoyed a heap of tedious and expensive transferring.

At this hour the tap room off the top deck of the ferry was almost empty, and some of the night owls weren't dressed much more fancy than he was. He was still feeling that last slug of bourbon he'd had out at the Presidio, so as he dropped his gladstone by the brass rail he put a spurred Justin up on the same and told the barkeep he'd try one of them new Coca-Cola drinks with ice, if they had it.

The barkeep didn't mind. He got the same nickel whether the drink he served was serious or not. But a burly gent just down the bar, who could have used a bath more than another slug of sloe gin, growled, "It has always been my considered opinion that a drugstore cowboy who drinks sodee water ain't man enough to piss standing up."

The barkeep warned, "Now, Turk, the gent ain't bothering you. So why would you want to bother him?"

The tough-looking Turk seemed to ponder the question before he replied thoughtfully, "I would say it was because it's the end of the week and my Indian blood is up. I boarded this fool ferry in quest of a nice friendly fight, and, damn it, I've rid it across the bay twice and nobody seems willing to fight me."

He grinned at Stringer, exposing a serious need of dentistry as well as soap as he asked hopefully, "How about it, cowboy? Would you be kind enough to fight with me if I let you take the first swing?"

Stringer smiled back. Turk was too drunk to read the cougar coldness in Stringer's normally friendly amber eyes as he told the bully, "I'd rather spend the rest of the night aboard a train than in a drunk tank, if it's all the same with you."

Turk shook his head stubbornly and insisted, "It ain't all the same with me. My Indian blood is up, and you're the only cuss in sight that looks as if he might be able to go one round with me."

Stringer sighed, picked up his gladstone, and carried his Coca-Cola out to the open promenade deck in his free hand, pretending not to hear as the ferocious drunk hurled unkind remarks about his mother at him.

It wasn't easy. Stringer's mother had died when he was still a kid. He was still mighty fond of her. But, as in the case of the gal on the second landing, there were temptations one just had to try to ignore in a world where temptation and troubles one couldn't avoid seemed so handy.

He walked back to the end of the ferry that was acting as the stern going this way across the inky waters of the bay. He put his gladstone down on a hardwood bench and stood by the rail to finish his Coca-Cola in private. He thought about the six-gun rig he'd packed along with his possibles in the nearby bag. He brushed the thought away. It might be fun to stroll back into the tap room wearing a double-action S&W .38 on his hip. But he'd get stared at enough, striding to the depot through downtown Oakland in just his faded riding outfit. One had to get a ways from big towns like San Francisco before folk considered a man wearing a gun rig properly dressed.

He finished the harmless drink and set the empty glass by his gladstone for now as he got out the makings for a smoke. He'd just finished sealing it with his tongue when something that was either a grizzly or a mighty strong man grabbed his shoulder to spin him around for a right cross.

Stringer's head wasn't there when Turk's heroic right cleft the air where his face had just been. As the burly bully threw a left hook, Stringer blocked it with his right forearm and counter-punched with his own left. It landed with a satisfying crunch that finished Turk's rotten front teeth for good, and, as the big brute staggered back to bounce off the inboard bulkhead, that should have been the end of it. But Turk bellowed, "Hot damn!" and came back for more, windmilling, since men that big and dumb seldom bothered to study even the basics of boxing.

Stringer stung him good a few more times. But the bigger man seemed too drunk, or too crazy, to let minor annoyances like a busted nose or blood all over his face slow him down. Stringer knew that the longer this kept up, the likelier Turk was to land one of those wild punches he kept throwing with little skill but pile-driver power. So he planted his heels and wound up to throw a punch of his own that he'd never have risked against a man who knew beans about boxing.

It landed. Turk never saw it coming. As Stringer's fist made a red ruin of Turk's face he staggered against the rail meant to be waist high to folk of average height and, catching it with his hip, went over the side, yelling one last uncalled-for remark about Stringer's mother before he hit with a mighty splash and the cold black waters of San Francisco Bay closed over him.

Stringer stared soberly at the receding patch of foam where the bully had gone under until he couldn't see it anymore. Then he muttered, "At least he could have *tried*," before he picked up the glass and gladstone to return to the tap room. As he placed the empty glass on the bar and asked how close they were now to the other side, the barkeep said, "We'll be there any minute. I was just about to send someone to warn you. That crazy drunk you were having trouble with said something about going out after you. I can see, thank God, he couldn't find you in the dark out there."

Stringer smiled thinly. "Just my luck. I always manage to miss all the fun. Was he really part Indian, like he said?"

The barkeep picked up the glass to rinse it as he shrugged and said, "Lord knows. He's sure a pest on this run. They say he used to be a bare-knuckles champ before liquor got to him. The cops on shore say they can't arrest him for us unless he really causes serious trouble on board. If you want my opinion, I think they're afraid of him. They say he busted up a paddy wagon bare-handed one time. I sure wish he'd fall over-board before he kills somebody."

Stringer chuckled. "Just keep wishing, then. You know what they say about wishes coming true if you wish hard enough."

Stringer got off at Los Molinos with his gun on his hip and goose bumps under his denim jacket. For it was well before dawn, and the autumn nights were cold in northern California. He'd just spent the good part of the night sitting up in the Oakland waiting room and then dozing fitfully aboard a passenger-freight combo that seemed to stop and start every few minutes in a series of heroic jolts. He was hungry, too.

Despite the hour the platform at Los Molinos was busy and fairly well lit by a string of Edison bulbs. Few passengers got on or off trains in the wee small hours, but a heap of freight did. Most of it was being unloaded this far up the line. He stood there a time with his glad-stone, scanning about for any sign of Joe Malliwah. The only two people in sight who didn't seem to be shifting crates and barrels looked Californio, or leftover Mex. An old man wearing a straw sombrero was tending a steam cart of what smelled like hot tamales. A pleasantly plump señorita with a serape thrown over her frilly cotton blouse and maroon fandango skirts was leaning against a pile of crates with a bored expression on her childlike face. Stringer felt sure he knew what she was selling. He drifted over to the tamale cart instead for breakfast.

The orange soda-pop the old geezer had for sale was awful, but nothing tasted better to a hungry man in predawn cold than a thick, juicy, homemade tamale wrapped in newspaper. He told the old man as much in Spanish. The old vendor was so pleased that he glanced about as if to make sure their secret was safe before he produced a thermos of real Arbuckle coffee and poured some into a tin cup for Stringer, murmuring, "That pop is barely fit for a dog to piss, and we Californios have to stick together. You did not learn Spanish in school or even Old Méjico, did you?"

Stringer chuckled and confided, "I was born and reared down the line in Calaveras County. Learning to talk to our neighbors was easier than fighting them, *viejo*."

They might have gotten to be even better pals, but then the gal in the maroon skirts drifted over, smiling uncertainly at the only man she'd seen getting down off the train. Stringer was about to tell her he was a happily married man when she asked him, in English, "Might you be the one they call Stringer?"

He admitted he might be, and she said, "I am Lola Malliwah. Joe sent me. Two good ponies wait for us across the way. Come. We should be out of town and on the trail before everyone wakes up and sees us together."

Stringer nodded, drained his cup and handed it back

with a *"Muchas gracias, viejo!"* and followed her as she dropped gracefully off the platform. As she led them away from the platform lights he could see her point. He couldn't see the two ponies tethered in front of a dark storefront until they were almost on top of them. But as she indicated that the pinto was his he asked her, "Why all the secrecy? And how come Joe sent you in place of himself?"

The Indian girl with the improbable name of Lola forked herself astride her own roan as she replied, "We are cousins. Joe had more than one good reason. To begin with, he is entered in a rodeo down at Weed for big prizes. He would have to let them keep his entry fee if he pulled out this late. His bigger and better reason is that, as you can see, I can pass for Mex. So far—and knock wood—the saltu where we are going have not shot at any Mexicans. They have some working for them in the Valley of Many-Colored Rocks. Joe is a full-blood and looks it. If you are spotted riding with me they might think you just picked up a puta in your travels. They are more likely to ask questions of another saltu and his fuck than to simply open fire, see?"

Having noted that the ponies seemed to have been trained by white wranglers, Stringer mounted his from the right side, which was the left unless was climbing up an Indian pony, and started to ask why in thunder he couldn't simply ride in openly, since the mining outfit seemed to be making no secret of their whereabouts. But she told him to shut up and ride. So he did until they were well out of town and seemed to be punching through chaparral instead of following any trace or trail. As they reined in atop a rise to rest their mounts a moment, Lola turned in her Spanish saddle to stare back the way they'd come. It gave Stringer a chance to repeat his question and add, "I only need a guide to get me somewhere near the mining settlement, Lola. They've wired the outside world for help against your people, no offense. So why should they act surly to a newspaperman just doing his fool job?"

It was too dark to read her expression, but she seemed to be frowning with her voice as she replied, "I thought you had come to help *us*, not *them*. Joe says you were good at picking off enemy snipers when you rode with him in Cuba. That is why we put a good rifle on that saddle for you."

Stringer had already noticed the Winchester stock bouncing against his right rump as they loped uphill. He smiled sheepishly and admitted, "I wasn't supposed to do that, down Cuba way. I was sent in as a war correspondent, and we weren't supposed to carry arms. But the Spaniards seemed to shoot at us a lot in any case, and, well, a man has a right to protect his fool self."

"Joe says you can blow a rabbit's head off at fifty yards. Joe says you fight good hand to hand as well. We did not send for you to talk to our enemies. We want you to kill them for us. Everyone already knows what they are doing on Yana land. We want them *off* Yana land, forever. Come, we can walk our ponies for now. Nobody seems to be trailing us. But we have far to go."

As Lola took the lead again, down the far slope, he noticed it figured to be rough and prickly as well as far. He protested, "I'd have brought some chaps, had anyone told me we'd be riding through the shrubbery so direct. As I read the map, that new company town of Quicksilver must be a good eighty miles from here as the crow flies. So how come we seem to be zigzagging through all this high chaparral so early in the game? If it was up to me I'd follow the regular roads at least as far as Mount Lassen and start my skulking from there."

"I know. That is why it has been so easy to avoid you saltu until recently. It is bad enough to make your way through the mountains on horseback, even if you stay off the trails. Horses can be seen and heard from far away. That is why you saltu have beaten all the Horse-Indians to the east. Even the Horse-Indians used to laugh at my kind and call them root diggers. But many of us are still here, living the true way, because we were never tempted to ride and fight in the saltu style against greater numbers and better weapons."

"Some Miwok kids I played with down to Calaveras County showed me how easy it was to lie doggo in the brush just off the trail and let our elders just ride past us. Miwok were a holy terror at Halloween, and I once got back at a mean teacher with some Indian lore. She usually caught the white kids who tipped over her out-house. They didn't know how to become invisible, like me and my Miwok pals. But, no offense, Miss Lola, ain't you and your cousin Joe living sort of off the blanket to be jawing about this pure way of yours?"

She sighed and said, "Our elders moved onto a reservation when we were little. The true way is hard, and the rations the BIA can be so free with are very tempting."

She seemed to consider her own words for a time as they rode on. Then she said, "Sometimes I miss the way we roamed when I was little. But coming in wasn't all bad. They taught us to speak saltu and even read and write it a little. I like to wear these clothes, during the cold moons at least, and we get to eat a lot more. The old free ways could be hungry ways, and while it was fun for the young and healthy, it was very hard on the old and sick. Sometimes I don't know which way is best. I like canned beans and soft white bread with butter and jam on it. But sometimes I feel a craving for yuna meal boiled with banhia fat, the way my mother made it when I was little."

He backed her up on the Yana words and she said, "Oh, I am sorry. I keep forgetting you are saltu. You speak so softly and polite. 'Yuna' are acorns. 'Banhia' means deer. There are oaks and deer on the reservation, but not enough for us to eat a lot of either. Preparing acorn meal to make it edible is hard work, and men content to stay on the reservation all the time are too lazy to hunt deer. Those with ambition, like Joe, go down to Fat Valley, where they can work for money now. One time Joe brought a whole side of elk he *paid* for to Grandfather Tetna. Have you ever heard of such a thing? Grandfather Tetna was very cross. But he ate all that elk meat just the same."

Stringer said that didn't sound too dumb and asked, "Might your grandfather be the old gent Joe told me about in his letter?"

"Yes. He has a new girlfriend, an old Yana woman who'd been chased out of the Valley of Many-Colored Rocks. Joe says he is glad. Old men can go crazy, jacking off all alone. Oh, damn, the sky to the east is starting to grow pale. I was hoping we could get farther away from any trail before we had to hide from the sun and those bad saltu."

Stringer frowned. "If there's a trail within a mile of here, the whites who laid it out admired steep grades. But I'd rather talk about your grandfather right now. If he's a reservation Yana and both you and Joe are living so white, how come your family is feuding with those mining men so far off in unclaimed country?"

She reined her pony through a clump of poison oak as she said, "Come. I know a nice campsite this way. I don't understand your questions about Grandfather Tetna. His new girlfriend is Yana. We are Yana. Even if the BIA has us down as Shasta, I think. The old woman who came to us wounded has a just injury to be avenged. Don't your people understand such customs?"

He sighed. "Some of us MacKails must have, back in their old country. My uncle Donald likes to brag about feuds we had with other clans over injuries going back so far that even the Scotchmen avenging them had lost track of who did what to whom and with what. As an American, I have to say the custom seemed more trouble than it could have been worth. The English never could have whupped us if we hadn't spent most of our energy at war with one another. But, now that you put things that way, I follow your drift. Blood is thicker than water, and a Yana is a Yana, even eating beans instead of acorns. I wonder if those mining men know what they've started. It might make more sense for me to tell them than to skulk about in the woods with your kinfolk. I hate to say it, Lola, but the map says that rough country betwixt Mount Lassen and the Nevada line is empty federal land, open to mining claims. We could be talking as much about a natural misunderstanding than malicious intent by either side."

She swore in Yana and said, "Don't call my grandfather's new girlfriend a liar. She follows the true way. Those saltu who came to spoil her gathering grounds knew people were there. They talked to some of them before they started to do bad things to them. I am not a stupid person. I know about mining claims. We had to move to the reservation when less cruel saltu claimed our best acorn grove as a gold mine. The Indian agent made them pay us to move. A copy of their claim was given to our chief, and it still hangs on the wall of our watt-goorwah. I'm sorry, I mean council house. It says the saltu have the right to dig up gold. I know what gold is. It says nothing about their having the right to dig up dead people. My cousin Joe says that even when saltu die they are buried with respect, and nobody is allowed to dig them up and laugh at their bones."

Stringer didn't answer. He knew how casual some whites could be about Indian burial grounds. It had always struck him as a sort of shitty way to look for pots and arrowheads. He doubted any mining outfit would be mining human bones as its main line of business. But perhaps some of their work force was in the market for mementos of their days out west. There was hardly a rail stop west of the Mississippi these days that didn't have a shop selling blankets, baskets, and machine-made moccasins. It was a shame some tourists couldn't seem to be content with such stuff. Nobody back east was likely to ask where you had picked up that cigar box full of arrowheads.

The sky above was just turning light enough to see colors by when they forged through a wall of fruit-laden manzanita and satin-barked madrone to find themselves in a sweet-smelling glen lined with soft sedge grass and feathery knee-high ferns. A little waterfall at the east rim of the natural bowl ran over a lip of black rock to fill a modest swimming hole of crystal-clear water. This emptied in turn via a little brooklet that snaked off to the west through a tunnel of tangled sedge and willow.

Lola reined in. "You are the first saltu who has ever seen this place. The sun cannot give us away here. Anyone riding the ridges around us will only see what seems to be a brush-filled canyon, too tangled to cross. We will stay here until wakara, I mean the moon, tells us it is safe to go on. Do you not find this place dambusah?"

"It's damn pretty, too," he said as he dismounted and led his pinto to the brooklet to tether it where it could both graze and drink at will. He saw she didn't worry as much about her roan. So as soon as she was off it he tethered it beside the pinto. He felt no call to chide her about her casual attitude toward her mount. A heap of romantic nonsense had been written to the contrary, but most Indians were rough on horses and mean as hell to their dogs, compared to white folk.

As he unsaddled both ponies, Lola asked him why, pointing out that they'd only be here until dark and that they'd just have to saddle up again at sunset. He said, "I can see your nation has been mighty pedestrian until recently. Call me a sissy if you will, but I just hate to ride a pony with saddle sores."

He dropped the saddles in the dry ferns up the slope a bit and began to rub both ponies dry with one of the saddle blankets as Lola rummaged in the saddlebags. She got out some canned goods and moved over by the edge of the pond to hunker down, calling, "Come. We dare not build a fire. But I chose canned food that can be eaten without cooking."

He hung both blankets over a branch to dry out. Then he hauled the Winchester from his saddle's boot and moved over to join her. "What's your hurry?" he asked. "We got all day to nibble and nap in this fool clearing. I'd have brought along a good book to read, had I known we'd be traveling this cautious. We can't be within seventy miles of that damned mining camp. So why are we acting like this was Apache country?"

She began to open a can of beans with a bowie and rather ominous skill as she replied, "This is enemy country to me. Joseph said to follow the true way all the way from Los Molinos. It is not our way to be seen by anyone as we move from place to place in a world so full of strangers. That is why so many of us still roam these mountains, unknown even to the BIA. Nobody can count you unless they can see you. Does that sound so strange to you?"

He said it did, adding, "Neither of us is wanted by the law, and even the Wild Bunch rides by daylight when they're not out to stick anyone up. Old Joe walked around natural when he was in the Army down Cuba way. Who in thunder could he be worried about way over here on the west side of Mount Lassen?"

She handed him an open can of beans as she replied, "It is better to be seen by no one than to find out too late that they are enemies. My cousin says you are famed among even your own people as a fighter. You have exposed a lot of bad saltu with your writings, too. How do you know the bad saltu we are after may not be expecting you? If *I* were a wicked person with bad deeds to hide, I would set a trap for you so that you could never tell on me."

He started to tell her how silly that sounded. Then he chewed some cold beans, swallowed, and said, "I did have trouble with a man last night, on the Oakland ferry, and, come to study on it, they did say he had Indian blood."

He swallowed some more and decided, "That won't

work. The fool Indians around here are supposed to be on my side. Even if old Turk was a bad breed, hired to head me off, there was no way the other side could have known just when I'd cross the bay aboard that ferry."

She naturally wanted to hear the whole tale. So he told her, leaving out the last part, which could get him in trouble if she blabbed about it to the wrong ears. She swallowed some of her own beans and said, "It sounds like my cousin could have been right. That mining company does have Mexicans and some wicked breeds working for it. No Yana, of course, but you know how bad Shoshone are. You say the man you fought with acted drunk but used to be a man who fought for prizes. What if they had him waiting in ambush across your trail?"

He started to say it seemed farfetched. Then he said, "Hmmm, they did say he'd been riding back and forth on the ferry a lot and I was the only one he finally picked a fight with. Anyone knowing I'd be coming up here from San Francisco would likely know I'd have to take that ferry sooner or later. But he packed no gun and . . . Right. He was big as a moose and may well have had me down as a sissy pencil pusher he could handle bare-handed. As a known local troublemaker, he'd have had to worry about the cops on either shore patting him down for weapons now and again. But I still like him best as just a crazy-mean drunk. It gets so damned Machiavellian your way."

She asked him what that big word meant. By the time he'd explained the sneaky ways of old Niccolò Machiavelli to her he was sorry he'd ever started. But she listened with interest, and when he'd set her straight she said, "I wish I knew that many big saltu words. But there is something I do not understand about you, Stringer. You know many big words, and you write for a big newspaper, yet when you talk, you sound like the other saltu cowboys my cousin rides with. The saltu teachers at the reservation school say it is wrong to say 'ain't.' Yet you say it without blushing. Do you write for your newspaper as you speak?"

He sighed and said, "Nope, and you ain't the first one who's asked me about that. 'Ain't' is a perfectly good Anglo-Saxon word, but you're right—my editor seems to think it's just awful. So I write in what's considered proper English. But I have no more reason to talk like that than Walter Scott had to say 'thee' and 'thou' when he sat down to supper. Can we get off the subject now? I just don't feel up to teaching the rules of grammer to a Yana gal right now."

She tossed her empty can away and said, "Good. Let's go swimming. That's more fun."

Then, as he gazed up at her slack-jawed, Lola sprang to her feet and proceeded to shuck her already immodest Mex outfit as if she thought she was the gal on the second landing.

Having seen both ladies bare-ass now, Stringer had to admit old Lola could give that model in San Francisco a run for the money when it came to naked curves. The Yana gal was shorter and plumper. So she curved even more as she gave a wild laugh and dove her tawny nude body headfirst into the pool, cutting the surface with next to no splash at all. He watched her dart off underwater like a sleek brown otter, and then he wondered what he was waiting for and just shucked his own duds to follow her into the clear clean water.

He was sure he'd made a dreadful mistake as the

water closed cold as ice around his own naked body.
But it felt better as the shock wore off, and the two of
them were soon splashing water and laughing at one
another like innocent skinny-dipping kids. It was easy to
feel innocent with your balls puckered back to boyhood
by snowmelt. He began to notice how numb the rest of
him was starting to get as well. So he called out, "I'm
getting out before I freeze to death, damn it!" and, suit-
ing actions to his words, he crawled out of the ice water
to flop face-down in the sun-warmed ferns. He was glad
he was lying face-down when Lola came out to flop
naked beside him, face-up. It was surprising how quick
a gent's privates could thaw out in the company of a
stark naked lady with a pretty little baby face.

"Your were right," she said. "It's too late in the autumn for much swimming. But wasn't that fun? Hold
me in your arms and warm me up a little, will you? I'm
still freezing."

He told her cautiously, "I'd sure like to, Lola. But to
tell the truth, I don't know how cool we'd be able to
stay if I did as you just asked."

She said simply, "I know. But I think fucking is fun
too, don't you?"

He laughed despite himself. "Since you put it that
way, I'll have to admit I've never found it painful. But
we have to study on how your cousin Joe might take it if
we were to, ah, follow this trail much farther."

She stared up at him innocently, her big sloe eyes
more confused than flirty. "Why? Joe has nothing to say
about my fucking. We are cousins. The way forbids us
from having fun together that way. Did you think you
had to ask him before you could fuck me?"

Stringer sighed, rose far enough to dust fern leaves

off his raging erection, and rolled atop her to put it
where they both seemed to want it. "Well, I won't tell
him if you won't," he said, and then she was wrapped
around him, bumping and grinding as she crooned to
him in her own lingo while he said some mighty nice
things in English, knowing promises made at times like
this didn't count as outright fibs.

She climaxed ahead of him in a natural, no-nonsense
way: to her way of thinking, sex was a simple pleasure
rather than a thing to worry about, like one's next meal
or getting a toothache no medicine man could do much
about. He was glad to oblige her as she begged for
more, and then, lest he tire before her, he let her get on
top. They were enjoying the best of both their worlds,
he knew, as he lay there in the ferns admiring the way
the dappled sunlight rippled on her smooth brown
bounding breasts. He was sophisticated about sex for a
white man, but still enough the product of his Edwar-
dian times to be excited by the sight of female nudity in
broad daylight; while she in turn found it exciting, if not
as shocking, to be taking such pale flesh up inside her.
Stringer was only suntanned where he generally wore no
pants. As she lovingly stroked his lower belly, she said,
"You look so soft and pale down here. But your belly is
so firm and hairy at the same time. How come you people don't pluck all you hair out down here as we do?"

"I don't know. Now that you mention it, a hairless
crotch does seem to have a lot of things going for it."
But she said she was glad he'd never plucked his pubic
hair, because it tickled her so much. So he rolled her
over in the ferns to get back on top and tickle her right.

There was no way, of course, to spend a full day at
even such fine rutting. So they slept for a spell, then

woke up to make love some more and swallow some tomato preserves she'd brought along. Then they went back to sleep, and the next time they woke up, the sky above their secluded love nest had turned pink and they were starting to get goose bumps. So they warmed up by making love again, and then it was time to wash off, bolt some more beans, and move on.

As they rode out of the little glen, Stringer picked some manzanita to nibble along the trail. They looked like bitty apples, and he didn't need her to tell him that manzanita would give you a bellyache if you ate too many of 'em. He said he just wanted to nibble on 'em from time to time in order to recall that pretty little clearing back there.

"Pretty is 'dambusah,' in my tongue. I think you are dambusah, too. Do not worry about forgetting the day we just had back there. The place where we must hide tomorrow is even nicer, and now that we are such good friends, we can get to some good fucking sooner."

CHAPTER
THREE

They sure could. The next few days and nights went a lot like Adam and Eve might have enjoyed exploring the Garden Of Eden before that snake messed up their heads. The western slopes of the Sierra Nevada, before so-called Christians came to mess it up, had been as close to a Garden Of Eden as the North American continent could come.

In what the Indians wistfully recalled as the Shining Times, at least five hundred nations with almost that many separate dialects had inhabited what was now the state of California more densely than it was inhabited at the moment. Though dismissed and despised as mere diggers by whites and more truculent Horse-Indians alike, Stringer knew that the Sierra tribes, at least, had led a far more sophisticated and prosperous existence than the true Desert Diggers of the barren Great Basin on the far side of his native range. In its pristine state, as it was up this way, the well watered western slope offered plenty of plump game-critters, from rabbit and quail to elk and bear. But the staple of the California tribes, and the secret of their ability to live at relative peace with one another in such great numbers, had been the acorn. Various species of oak trees grew like weeds from sea level up to the evergreen line of the higher crests to the east and all of them, from the dwarfed chaparral oak to the giant valley oak bore acorn crops for the gathering.

Whites who'd bothered to try eating an acorn tended to think this only served to prove how miserable and primitive the damned old Diggers were. For as every Anglo-Saxon since Robin Hood could tell you, acorns were just plain inedible, and, like the olive and banana, they were as they came off the tree. Olives had to be cured in brine, and banana stalks had to be ripened off the tree before anyone could eat them without getting mighty sick. Acorns required even more sophisticated treatment before they were fit for anyone but a rooting hog. But once Indian women had ground the bitter acorns to a course meal, leached their tannic acid out with endless rinsings, or suspended their acorn baskets in a running stream for a day or more, the results tasted a lot like ground chestnuts and could be boiled as a tasty mush or baked like bread.

The men and boys had done the hunting while the women and girls had gathered acorns, along with berries in season and a dozen or more varieties of onionlike bulbs. "Digging" was a mite more sophisticated than it looked. A lot of white settlers had tried it and wound up eating death camas, deadly snakeroot, or poisonous mushrooms, albeit only once. Stringer had learned as a boy, from Miwok neighbors, how to rustle up a pretty good free lunch along Manzanita Creek, down home in the Mother-Lode country, even though hydraulic mining had spoiled the best digging and Uncle Don's cows tended to get at the good stuff first. So Lola was surprised the time he rolled off her in yet another little clearing to pull up some onion grass to go with her beans and his tobacco. She was even more surprised when he plucked some jewelweed later to rub over their bare bodies. She giggled and said it tickled. He kissed her and explained he just hated to itch from poison oak and that they'd sure passed through enough of it by now. She pulled him down against her bare breasts, pouting her lower lip as she told him in a mocking way, "I thought I had a saltu boyfriend. Now I see you are at least part Yana."

"It was a Miwok gal I once went swimming with who showed me how to avoid oak itch, as a matter of fact. My own saltu elders showed me how to keep from getting lost in the high country. They'd learned that before they left the old country, being highlanders to begin with. You seem to be leading me in circles, Lola. Even by moonlight you can see the snows of the mountain you call Waw-gamupah and we call Lassen from many a rise, and, no offense, your star sisters tell me the same tale about the odd way you've been leading me. I enjoy a sort of outdoor shack-up as much as any man, but would you mind telling me why we don't seem to be getting anywhere important?"

She said she was too hot to talk about it right now. So he made love to her a spell and then repeated the question. She sighed and said, "You have a mean memory, don't you? I was hoping you might not notice. I would rather make love than explain the ways of my wild cousins. They do not think as you, or even me."

He insisted, "We're not screwing at the moment. Explain why we're wandering around up here so casual, damn it."

She sat up, brushing a clump of five-finger fern from her love-damp naked belly as she said, "We dare not go any farther on horseback. It would be almost as dangerous moving in the rest of the way on foot without a guide who knows just where the bad saltu from that mining camp patrol. As you guessed, I have been moving us back and forth with the snow cone of Waw-ga-mupah behind us. By this time the real people should have spotted us. When they feel like talking to us, they will come to us. Can I get on top now?"

He shook his head and said, "The notion of a naked Indian aiming an arrow at my naked ass has sort of cooled my desire for the moment. Are you saying we have to wander about like lost kids until we're ambushed friendly? How are the Yana up this way supposed to know we're on their side? When we have our duds on, I look like any other strange white man, and you could pass for Mex, no offense."

She nodded. "I have been thinking about that. Maybe it would be better if I braided my hair the old way and went naked above the waist from now on. If they took us for a saltu in the company of a Yana girl, and saw you were not cruel to me, they would come closer. Joe says that old Yana woman sent word to her band that a brave wanasee was on his way to help them. She may have neglected to tell them you were a saltu. They could be expecting an Indian called Stringer. Hoksah, that must be it."

Stringer sat up in the knee-high ferns, feeling more naked than he had when he'd flopped down in them with Lola to begin with. He had a good look-see at the surrounding wall of canyon oak and mountain bay, even though experience and common sense told him you never saw an Indian in the shrubbery unless he wanted you to see him. He muttered, "This is a hell of a way to run a railroad. We'd better get dressed."

"Why? The sun still smiles down on us warmly, and it won't be dark enough to ride for many hours."

He reached for his nearby jeans as he insisted, "We're in no fit condition to receive callers. Don't you have some way to signal any Indians about that it's all right for them to come calling, Lola?"

She shook her head and began to braid her long black hair. "No. Any smoke or noise we made would be heard by the bad saltu as well. The Yana are a quiet people. They cut down trees by chewing the wood with beaver-tooth knives because the sound of an ax carries far among these hills. They know we are here. We just have to give them time to make up their minds about us, see?"

He shook his head as he hauled on his boots. "Last night there was a whiff of snow in the air before dawn. We don't have all that much time before this nice Indian summer comes to a blizzardy halt. I grew up in the Sierra Nevada, honey, and *nevada* means snow in Spanish. We got enough of the stuff down south in Calaveras County. You have to get more up here."

She laughed. "Su-wah, but we have plenty of time before the snow moons come."

He shook his head again as he buttoned his shirt. "I've noticed your folk don't go in for clocks all that much. But the time to gather news is while it's happening. If you and your kin want the *San Francisco Sun* to run an exposé on that rough-and-ready mining outfit, it'll have to be soon, not next year, after both sides have spent the winter snowed in and not able to do all that much to each other even if they wanted to."

He rose to his feet and strapped on his gun rig. Lola just sat there bare-ass, braiding her hair. When she saw him don his jacket and old Rough Rider hat she asked where he thought he was going in the daylight. "Maybe up to the next ridge," he said. "I know some Miwok hand signals. It's worth a try. Your way is just too slow."

She told him he was being silly and went on braiding her hair as Stringer strode up out of the glen and worked east until he had a view of the apparently empty valley beyond. Way off to his right, on the valley floor, some manzanita branches were moving just a little. He knew Indians were more careful than that, and that deer just loved manzanita fruit. He was looking for a high point he could signal from with the sky behind him when he heard the sound of steel on stone and froze where he was, with his back to a bay tree. He knew Yana rode no ponies to begin with, let alone a steel-shod pony. He drew his .38 and stared hard in the direction of the distant sound, waiting to see what came next.

What came next was that a Winchester snicked to full-cock to his left and he was told in English to drop his damned gun. So he did. As his S&W crunched in the forest duff at his feet, Stringer turned, hands polite, to face the two white men who'd circled and suckered him on foot. They were dressed like a pair of saddle tramps. One was covering him with the Winchester,

which seemed reasonable, while the other was covering
him with a bow and arrow, which didn't. Stringer
smiled thinly at them and asked, "Are we playing cowboys and Indians?"

The one with the carbine nodded. "You might say
that, Stringer. It's your own fault for being so nosy.
Now, sad to say, we're going to have to carry you into
Quicksilver after finding you arrowed and scalped up
here in the hills."

Stringer blinked. "I sure hope you boys are just
greening me."

Then the one with the archery set let fly his arrow.

It missed by a yard. That was way too close for
Stringer's comfort. But as the would-be Indian nocked
another arrow to his bowstring he swore and said,
"Hell, let's just shoot him and shove arrows in the bullet
holes, Mike."

The one called Mike muttered, "Try again, at least
once." So the one with the bow drew it back again as
Stringer tensed to make a dive for his gun and at least
go down trying.

But then other arrows were humming in out of no-
where, aimed better, and as one dropped Mike another
hit the white bowman in the back so his own arrow
thunked into the gray bark high above Stringer's head.
Then it got very quiet. Stringer stared soberly down at
the two white men sprawled face-down on the leaf litter
with both their backs nicely pincushioned with reed
arrows. It seemed a piss-poor time to bend over for his
own gun, so he just stood there until a half-dozen Indians materialized from the surrounding chaparral. They
wore fringed deerskin breech clouts and little else save
for beads and otter-hide arrow cases. Their bows were

compounded of juniper wood and elk sinew. He was pleased to note that none of them seemed to be aimed his way. But a couple were still nocked with arrows. One of the Yana addressed him in what might as well have been bird chirps. Stringer smiled as friendly as he could manage and tried, "No savvy Yana."

That didn't seem to be getting them anywhere until he heard what sounded like "Stringer" among the bird chirps. He patted his own chest and tried, "Hoksah, me Stringer."

That seemed to work better. One of the Indians came over to pick up his S&W and hand it to him. As Stringer put it back in its holster, the Indian pointed northeast, and while the words meant nothing his meaning was clear. Stringer said, "Hold on. I left one gal and two ponies down yonder the other way."

But the Indian who'd just saved his hide repeated the demand in a firmer tone. So Stringer saw he had little choice in the matter until he could find some fool Yana who savvied English.

That was easier said than done. The warrior band he'd met up with were legged-up better than Prussian infantry. Every time Stringer tried to pause on a ridge for breath they nudged him on until it felt as if they'd marched him at least all the way to Nevada. Stringer was in good shape for a white man, but his high-heeled Justins had never been designed for skipping over hill and dale along no trail at all as far as he could see. They moved him upslope at quick-march and made him double-time downslope until, just before he felt sure he was about to drop in his tracks, they bulled through a wall of madrone and poison oak to run him into a hole in the ground.

It was a lava-tube cave, he saw, once they were inside it. The volcanic Mount Lassen to the west had never blown its top in human memory, but Stringer still hoped it wouldn't decide to erupt for another year or so. That was about the only thing that hadn't gone wrong since he'd received that pesky letter from Joe Malliwah, and Lassen *was* a volcano, when one studied on it.

The once molten rock walls of the long but low-slung cave were cool and shiny black glass now. Stringer saw the glow of firelight ahead, and when his guides—captors or whatever—led him around it he saw even more Indians: men, women, and children gathered around a stone circle filled with mostly glowing coals and a few flickering blue flames. He knew manzanita roots burned like that. Nobody but the kids stared at him. But they must have known they had company. An old man wearing a rabbit-strip robe dipped two fingers in the pot of acorn mush in front of him and shot Stringer a questioning glance. Stringer had been taken home for supper by Miwok in his schoolboy days, so he knew enough to nod and rub his stomach as he hunkered down across from the old man.

A pretty, moon-faced little gal served Stringer a watertight basket of mush with a smile and no spoon. Stringer dipped two fingers in, tasted, and tried, "Achoo chubb," which meant it was good, he hoped, and that made all the Yana smile and get down to the business of eating.

The acorn meal base of the stew gave it a wild piney substance, while the bits of quail and rabbit stirred in gave it flavor. He knew there'd be at least a little deer liver in the stew if they were hunting more freely during the last good hunting moons. Joe had said the white intruders had fucked up the Yana way of life in these parts.

He wished there was some way he could make them understand he understood. He knew that while the higher ridges of the Sierra furnished some hunting and gathering, the lower mountain meadows were where the good stuff came from. Though not exactly farmers, the Sierra tribes had depended, in the Shining Times, on what amounted to yearly crops of nature's bounty, gathered at different times of the year from different parts of their ranges. Sweet toyon berries and spring bulbs grew best near running water in the valleys between dryer ridges. Nobody caught many trout or salmon on the higher slopes, either. With winter coming on, the deer would be moving down to the flat valley floors, and elk seldom grazed anywhere else. This acorn mush would taste a lot richer, he knew, if the women had gathered the nuts from fat valley oaks instead of scrubbier canyon oak, as they'd no doubt had to. He could see why they wanted their valley back. Skulking up here in the hills offered mighty few luxuries, and it figured to be cold as hell as well come winter, when the sensible way for Indians to live was in an earth-covered lodge close to a handy stream and sheltered from the raw winds that could likely whistle through this glass cave like it was a big old flute. But the hell of it was, he had no way to help folk he couldn't even talk to. He'd picked up a bare handful of Yana words and phrases from old Lola, and, try as he might, he just couldn't make them savvy that he had a fine translator handy if only they'd let him go back and fetch her.

He knew Lola was likely worried about him by now.

Sooner or later she'd track him to that bay tree, only to find two white men stretched out stiff with arrows in their backs. There was an outside chance she'd read what happened and track him and his new pals here. It was even more likely she'd turn tail and ride for her life. Lola was a reservation gal who might not know any more than he did about really wild Indians. Most women who et jam on bread were inclined to act spooked at the sight of blood in any case, and—damn it!—she had that Winchester he felt sure he'd have better use for.

The bland meal around the fire went on and then some. Yana seemed to enjoy conversation with their supper. He didn't even know how to turn down second helpings. So he had to eat 'em when the gal serving him noticed he'd finished his first basket.

A hundred years or so later, while the women and children got to eat what was left, the old chief belched politely and got out a stone-bowled pipe. Stringer knew what odd substitutes for tobacco the Sierra tribes favored. So when the pipe was passed around to him he shoved a wad of Bull Durham into the half-done bowl. The results still tasted awful when he took a polite draw on the pipe, but the Indians seemed to think he'd just done them a swell favor. They kept saying his tobacco was *achoo chubb* and even *dambusah*. Stringer could only opine they were damned right.

He was hoping he wouldn't have to smoke any more tobacco mixed with wild cherry bark and mayhaps lizard tails when he heard a commotion behind him and turned to see Joe Malliwah, of all gents, coming to join them in his cowhand duds.

As Joe sat down beside Stringer he grunted, "You was supposed to meet me in Los Molinos, you asshole. How come you didn't?"

"How come? Didn't you send your cousin Lola to pick me up?"

Joe answered some questions the old chief shot at them before he said, "I have no cousin called Lola. Is that the woman you've been screwing all over these hills for the past few days?"

Stringer replied, in an injured tone, "You sure read sign dirty. Never mind why she seemed so friendly. Who the hell was she if she wasn't kin to you, damn it?"

"I don't know. They told me in Los Molinos that you rode out of town with a Mex gal. Whatever she was, she knew how to leave a tough trail to follow, even on horseback. I could only trail the two of you by daylight. Every time I caught up with you you'd screwed her some more and moved on. After a time I could see you'd made it almost this far, but that you both seemed to be lost. You were riding back and forth, going no-place. Then I met a Yana brother who told me they had saved you from those bastards from Quicksilver and brought you here. Do you have any idea what might be going on?"

"Yep. And now I know how old Samson must have felt when he woke up with that short haircut. I was supposed to be carried into that mining camp as another victim of you vicious redskins, arrowed and scalped. Lucky for me, it takes some practice to shoot an arrow worth a damn."

"My Yana brothers told me about the saltu with a Paiute bow. Hear me, Stringer, that woman must have set you up."

Stringer nodded soberly. "I just said that. She was so soft and friendly-acting, too. But then, Samson might never have fallen for Delilah if she'd come at him mean and ugly. I see now that she was sent to head me off and lead me astray. But after that it gets murky. She claimed to be Yana. She even spoke Yana, and anyone can see she knows her way about these hills. So why would a Yana gal be working in cahoots with the enemies of her own tribe?"

"She wouldn't," Joe said flatly. "Not if she was a real Yana. How do you know she was? Do you speak the lingo?"

Stringer agreed he didn't, but offered a few words and phrases the mysterious little gal had used along the trail. His try made some of the Yana women giggle, and the kids all laughed right out.

"She was trying to fool you with some baby-talk Yana she picked up somewhere," Joe said. "Yana is not an easy lingo to learn. So trust me when I say you could teach me Scotch-Gaelic before I could teach you Yana."

Stringer smiled thinly. "I'd have me a time teaching anyone The Gaelic. I know a few words and how to cuss in it, but the grammar is a real bitch and hardly worth the effort when you consider how many still talk it."

His Indian mentor nodded. "Yana may be more complicated. For openers, Yana men and women put different endings on their words to show whether a man or woman is speaking."

Stringer frowned. "For Pete's sake, can't they tell just by looking? I know it's none of my business, but hardly any of these gals have their tits covered."

"Don't stare at them," Joe warned. "My people are very modest, in their own way. Yana men never stare at women unless they are interested in them. The woman you were with let you have her the first place you camped. No real Yana woman would give herself to a man she had only just met. She used the male verb endings when she spoke baby-talk Yana to you. No Yana would have been fooled by her for one second."

"Don't rub it in. Help me figure out why she treated me so dirty, damn it."

Joe suppressed a smirk. "Maybe she *liked* to act dirty. The two of you were sure rough on the ferns. They sent her to lure you into that ambush so they could blame it on this band. She had to get you there first, and maybe she enjoyed her work as she kept trying to make you trust her."

Stringer smiled ruefully. "I know *I* sure enjoyed it," he admitted. "I did get to wondering, though, toward the last, why she was leading me no place in particular. But being the fool I am, I never suspected downright treachery, and I still can't grasp the infernal motive behind so much effort. The mining outfit sent out a call for help, saying they were being attacked by wild Indians, no offense. They must have known newspapermen would come in with the Army, right?"

Joe Malliwah shrugged. "You were not on your way here with any troops. You were coming alone. You have a rep for being a smarter-than-usual newspaperman. You have exposed many crooks in your time. I think that if *I* were a crook I would not want a newspaperman like you anywhere near me."

Stringer reached absently for his makings, remembered in time that he couldn't smoke alone in such company, and got out a match stem to chew instead as he mused aloud, "Well, they just might have tried to set me up on the Oakland ferry, and they surely had old Lola head me off at Los Molinos. But no matter how it looks to you and these evicted kin of yours, there's nothing all that crooked about staking a mineral claim on public land. They've incorporated their company town of Quicksilver as a part of Lassen County, fair and square as far as white man's law sees it. They've outright admitted having trouble with a local Indian band the BIA didn't even know about. I don't think the Army will be coming, unless things get a lot worse. The BIA will likely send an Indian agent in, perhaps next spring, and if he's an at all decent cuss he may chide the rougher mining men for mistreating his new wards. Do I have to tell a full-blood how often a white man hangs or even goes to jail for using an off-the-reserve and no-doubt savage Indian for target practice?"

Joe Malliwah seethed a spell before he growled, "I wrote to you because you say things as they are, with no sugar coating. I know how little they have to worry about abusing these people. They must be up to something even you saltu would send them to jail for doing."

He turned to speak Yana for a time with the others. The old chief nodded and got out a beaver-tail pouch and began to dig into it. At last he produced a lump of stone that looked a lot like a wad of cinnamon toast. He handed it across to Joe, who showed it to Stringer. "This is the kind of rock they seem to be most interested in. They chased away the family who lived near an outcrop of this paint-stone the first day they came. It is not gold ore. I know what gold ore looks like. Do you think they may be mining something they don't want you to know about?"

Stringer held the lump up to the light, just to be polite, as he said, "No. This is cinnabar. Mercury ore. They'd never have staked a mercury claim and named their town Quicksilver if they wanted to mine mercury in secret."

Joe translated and asked if this mercury stuff was as important to the saltu as the gold that drove them crazy.

Stringer shook his head. "Not hardly. It's valuable. Worth about the same as silver, depending on the market. They don't use or need near as much mercury as silver, so most of the time it's worth less. As quicksilver, it's used mostly to make thermometers and play tricks with in chemistry classes. It's used more in chemical compounds. The firing caps of the bullets in our guns are made partly of mercury. They brew some medicines from it too. Tell these folks not to try that. Some mixtures of mercury are poisonous as hell."

"What if those crooks are planning to poison us?" Joe asked.

To which Stringer could only reply wearily, "They don't have to go to that much trouble, Joe. We just agreed they have what amounts to a hunting license on these unregistered Yana. They were fixing to kill me more crudely just this afternoon. Give the old gent's medicine stone back and let's study on how we can get his band on the BIA rolls."

Joe Malliwah shook his head. "They don't want to be agency Indians. My grandfather has already suggested that to them. They say they would rather die free than become the dogs of the saltu."

"Did your grandfather tell them we don't eat near as many dogs as they might? I want to help them, Joe. I might be able to get them a fair shake if we run a nice sad story about Lo, the poor Indian. But until and unless you can get 'em to meet us halfway, those mining company toughs are just going to go on defending white civilization from howling savages, if you follow my drift."

"Sure I follow your drift," Joe said. "I'm a cowboy these days, but I'm still Indian enough to tell you that they don't understand meeting anyone halfway. Sometimes I have a heap of trouble understanding it myself, and, hell, I *like* jam on white bread."

CHAPTER
FOUR

Having learned little that he hadn't already known about the mining operation in the Valley of Many-Colored Rocks, Stringer asked Joe Malliwah to tell the Yana how swell he thought their stew had been and headed for the entrance of their cave. Nobody tried to stop him, but Joe tagged along, insisting over and over again that Stringer was *dawanah*.

As they got outside, Stringer said, "Let me see if I have it straight. 'Dambusah' means pretty and 'da-wanah' means crazy?"

Joe growled, "You've always been pretty crazy. This is the first time you've threatened suicide. Hear me. You can't go into that mining camp now."

"Sure I can. Now that I know where I am, it figures to be mostly downhill, and I ought to make it just the other side of sundown."

"Alone and on foot? At least let me go with you. We

can ride my pony double, and two guns are better than one."

Stringer shook his head. "I wouldn't show my pale face in town if I had a lick of sense. But I've yet to get a good story by acting shy. If everyone in Quicksilver were out to get me, those guys wouldn't have had to act so sneaky. They'd have just waited for me to ride in for a public execution. I know this may be hard to sell to an Indian, Joe, but all of us ain't bad, and some of us can act downright decent. Decent or just sensible, I don't think the town law could be in on it. They were the ones who called for help, and even if they've changed their minds for some fool reason, no lawman with a jail at his disposal has to lay for unwelcome strangers in the woods. Some other gents in town may be surprised to see me, though. I can't wait to see the expression on their faces."

Joe glanced up through the tree branches above them. "You'll never make it before dark."

"That's even better. If I stroll into town along that wagon trace like an innocent big-ass bird, I figure to be in town and surrounded by witnesses before anyone notices."

He looked for the sun to get his bearings and started walking. Joe tagged along afoot to make sure he didn't get lost again.

A while later, as they stood in a saddle, staring down into the valley beyond, Joe pointed at some lights winking on already as the valley filled with purple shadows. "That's Quicksilver. They've put up more buildings since the last time I scouted it. You could make it before sundown if you bee-lined straight down from here."

Stringer pointed off to the west, where two thin lines

of bare dirt wound snakelike through the hills around the little mining town. "Anyone on the prod for an Indian attack would be dumb not to shoot first and ask questions later if they spied me coming down from the high country in this tricky light. I'd best come calling polite from the direction of more civilized parts. You wait for me back near that lava tube, and if I don't wind up dead I'll get back to you when and if I figure out some answers."

They shook on it and Stringer started working his way west through the high chaparral. By the time he got down to the wagon trace, smelling like a cross between a drugstore and a cedar love chest, the sun had set, outlining the ominous bulk of old Mount Lassen in ruby light.

He headed the other way, not trying to muffle the crunch of his boot heels as he strode along a wagon rut. He'd walked a little less than a mile when out of a dark clump of roadside oak came a call demanding who the hell he thought he was and where the hell he thought he was going.

Stringer called back, "Hold your damned fire. If I were any whiter I'd be an albino. I lost my mount a ways back, and they told me there was a mining camp around here somewhere. I don't feel up to walking anywhere more important."

The voice that had challenged him became more friendly as it replied, "Come on in closer. You sure don't sound like an Indian. Quicksilver is private property, but I reckon the company won't mind, as long as you come in peace."

As Stringer joined the two shadowy figures under the oaks he could just make out their mail-order badges and rifle barrels by the last light of dusk. One of them struck a match and shoved it in Stringer's face. He shook it out and said, "Sorry. We had to make sure. They say the Comanche used to trick folk with rascals speaking pure American."

Stringer nodded. "They used Army bugle calls as well. But ain't you boys taking a less serious tribe sort of serious?"

The one who'd lit him up for inspection replied, "Company orders. Diggers may not be much next to Comanche or Sioux, but an Injun is an Injun, and the Good Lord seems to have created 'em equal when it comes to sneaky tricks."

The other one said, "You might still make the funeral in town if you hurry. Couple of old boys got arrowed in the hills just a few hours back. They said they was riding out to see if they could find any Indians."

His comrade said, "They found 'em. The kid they took along to hold their ponies brung 'em in a spell back, riding face-down across their saddles. You say the Diggers got your pony too, cowboy?"

Stringer replied, "Can't say for sure. I left my mount tied to a madrone one time, went off to gather some firewood, and I never saw the poor critter again. Might have been a plain old horse thief, you know."

Neither one seemed to buy that notion. One said flatly, "It was Diggers. No white man straying far off the beaten path would last all that long in these hills, honest or otherwise. You're lucky they only lifted your pony."

"I'd best get on into town, then. You boys would know better than me whether the law in these parts might be watching out for white owlhoots, right?"

The one who'd flashed the match in his face said, "We'd be arresting you instead of talking to you if we'd been told to guard this road against anyone but Indians."

Stringer agreed that that sounded sensible and moseyed on, feeling a heap less ill-at-ease. He'd guessed right about the town law. They didn't seem to be in on it. But he still had to find out what in thunder somebody around here was so worried about his noticing.

The town, if one wanted to call it that, was only a quarter mile up the wagon trace. The lights along the one main street outlined a closer black mass of the mining layout itself. It was easy to make out a smelter stack spewing smoke up at the stars. He passed a loading platform with a swamping road tractor and some freight wagons parked nearby. He didn't go closer for a better look. If they had a night watch posted out along the road, they were sure to have someone riding shotgun over their more serious property. He'd already noticed there was no spur track out of the valley. The smelter and road tractor explained that well enough. Raw ore was too bulky to haul out by wagon. But cinnabar was easy to process on site, and while pure mercury was heavy as hell, you could load a mighty valuable amount of it in steel bottles on a wagon. It was a gut-and-git operation. They meant to mine and process that one outcrop until it petered out or got expensive to skim and then, in the sweet bye-and-bye, just give the valley back to the Indians in a messed-up condition the Indians might not have much use for.

As he passed the mining mess, he was suddenly aware of the water-filled ditch running alongside the road. It had to be what they'd left of the mountain stream nature had put there to drain the valley. As he crossed a footbridge over the inky water he didn't have to sniff hard to tell what they'd done to the local fishing. The fetid ditch stank of animal, vegetable, and mineral crud. A mining company that couldn't afford a rail line could hardly be expected to spring for water treatment. What the Yana had once used as a trout stream was now an open sewer.

He walked on to what was apparently the center of town. The company store had closed for the night, but the company saloon was still open. Stringer parted the batwing doors and went on in warily until he saw he and the barkeep seemed to have the place all to themselves. Stringer bellied up to the bar, ordered a beer, and tried to sound casual as he asked where everyone else was.

The barkeep filled a schooner for Stringer as he asked, "Where have you been? Didn't they tell you about the funeral tonight?"

Stringer said, "I did hear something about a couple of old boys getting arrowed this afternoon. I can't say they were pals of mine, though."

The barkeep said, "I barely knowed 'em either. But if I wasn't on duty I'd feel duty-bound to pay my last respects to fellow white men. They was a couple of sheriff's deputies, sent over from Quincy by the county to give us a hand with the damned old Diggers. What am I supposed to do with this silver dollar, damn it?"

Stringer glanced down at the coin he'd placed on the fake mahogany between them. "I was hoping you'd give me some change back," he said. "If beer costs more than a dollar a glass in this town, I may just join the WCTU."

The barkeep explained, "Beer is a nickel a schooner

here, in company scrip. I'm not supposed to deal in U.S. cash."

Stringer smiled thinly. "I can see how paying folks real money could confuse their immigrant heads. But I don't work here. Do you want me to puke back the couple of swallows I've already downed?"

The barkeep glanced around, confirming that this was a private conversation, then said, "That sounds messy. Suppose I just put this silver away and you drink moderate or slip me an extra quarter now and again should I ask you."

Stringer said that sounded fair. He wasn't surprised when the barkeep picked up the dollar and put it in his own pocket. He sipped some more suds before he said, "Correct me if I'm wrong, but I was just about sure that the county seat was Susanville. Ain't Quincy the seat of Plumas county, to the south?"

The mining company man shrugged. "It could be. What difference does that make?"

"We're in Lassen County, unsurveyed a part as this may be. The sheriff of Plumas County has no jurisdiction this far north. So why would he be sending deputies up here?"

The barkeep thought, then said, "All I know is that he did. Mayhaps the law ain't all that picky when it comes to Indians. Us white men got to stick together, you know. Let me put another head on that beer afore the place fills up again."

He did so as he either bragged or bitched, "This town ain't four months old and we already got a graveyard started. Poor little Mary-Jo Crocker died just last month, and now we got them two poor old boys massacred by Indians. It just goes to show that even in life we're in the midst of death."

"I'm sorry about the gal. How did she die?"

"Death camas, according to the doc. She was only eight years old and must have thought she was picking wild onions. You should have seen her folks carry on. She was their only child, the poor little thing. I got to go to her funeral. She looked like she was asleep."

Stringer drank some more beer and said soberly, "Death camas can have that effect. Are you saying that one kid and the two cusses they're just planting make up the grand total of dead whites since this valley was settled by whites?"

The barkeep nodded but asked, "Hell, how many folk do you want to see dead in just four months? Are you some kind of homicidal lunatic?"

"Not hardly. But I was told you were having Indian trouble up here. Do you call one child getting into death camas an Indian uprising?"

The barkeep shot him an injured look and opined, "I surely do. We've had almost a dozen folk hit or at least grazed with arrows and twice that many scared skinny by their howling and hell-raising. They've busted windows and cut clotheslines and even tipped an outhouse over with an old woman sitting in it. The poor old gal come close to dying of fear and mortification. Them Diggers are mean as hell."

"I was told you got some of them amid all the fussing," said Stringer, one eyebrow cocked.

The barkeep smiled smugly. "That we did. Rifle shots carry a heap further than arrows. The boys nailed six or eight of the red rascals for sure. Some others they winged likely crawled off to die later in the chaparral.

None of 'em was buried in hallowed ground, though. You don't have to bury Indians. If their kin don't come for 'em after dark, the coyotes will."

"So I've heard. But somebody told me your outfit was digging up Indians that had been dead a mite longer. Weren't they interested in fresher specimens?"

The barkeep looked blank for a moment. Then he laughed. "Oh, that ain't Consolidated Minerals. You're talking about some scientific jaspers camped just outside the east end of town. They been collecting skulls for some museum back east. I can't say whether they collected any recent Indian heads. Sounds sort of messy, if you ask me. One of 'em who drops by here now and again says they like old bones best. Don't ask me why."

Stringer promised he wouldn't and asked if there was a Western Union office in town. The barkeep shook his head. "Nope. There's a company wire to the outside, if the Diggers ain't cut it again. It's private, but you might ask, come morning. The telegraph set would be locked away for the night at this hour."

Stringer finished his schooner, said he'd be back later for some more, and left. Even if the larcenous barkeep forgot the credit he still had coming on that cartwheel, Stringer felt a beer and a half was worth a whole dollar when you threw in the information he'd been served with it.

The street outside was more crowded now as the mine workers and their women drifted down from the hillside funeral service. Stringer knew he had plenty of time to ask where a stranger might bed down for the night. He wanted to talk to as many folks as he could before they went on home. He passed a smithy and some dark storefronts, and then, sure enough, he spied some tents up ahead, lit from inside. He saw a shapely shadow moving inside the nearest one. Then a female figure came outside to toss a pan of dishwater on the ground and let it run wherever it had a mind to.

Before she could turn away, Stringer hailed her and asked if she might know where the scientific expedition might be.

"You've found it. I'm Nancy Gore. My father is Dr. Gore of the California Institute of Anthropology. Father just turned in for the night after a hard day's fieldwork. Is there anything I might do for you?"

As he got closer, Stringer saw there surely was. But he didn't think the willowy ash blonde in riding breeches and a mighty thin silk blouse could have meant that the way he wished he could take it. He ticked the brim of his Rough Rider hat and said, "My name's MacKail. I ride for the *San Francisco Sun,* ma'am. I was sent up here to do a feature on the local Indians, and, seeing you seem so interested in 'em . . ."

She smiled. "Heavens, Father isn't interested in the miserable Diggers around here. His thesis is that a far superior race once inhabited these mountains. I don't want to wake him up, but I'll be happy to show you some of the things we've discovered, if you'll follow me."

He did. She looked pretty from that point of view as well. She led him into a darkened tent and struck a match to light the bright Coleman lantern. He was sort of sorry she'd done that as he stared soberly down at a trestle table covered with grinning skulls, stone tools, and bits of busted crockery. But she seemed to take pride in the collection as she told him, "A lot of the remains we've found seem to be recent, more debased types. But these prime specimens prove this valley was once inhabited by a handsome race with the brain capacity of superior whites. Have you ever seen such strong and graceful bone structure?"

"Yep. Indians don't bury their dead as deep as we do. Some don't bury 'em at all. How come you had to go to all this trouble to measure Indian skulls, ma'am? They got boxes and boxes of Indian bones in the Smithsonian back east. Nobody's ever had time to measure a tenth of 'em. Seems to me it would make as much sense, and upset the local Yana less, if you were to just work with bones cluttering every museum in the country."

She shot him a superior look. "Don't be silly. The extinct Yana were unique to these hills, and it could hardly upset any of them now."

"You're wrong," he said flatly. "The Yana don't know they're extinct. They moved into this valley within living memory. So what you have here as a superior race are just Yana with bigger heads, dead no more than fifty or sixty years. The ones you seem to have dismissed as Diggers are just their smaller relatives— their relatives who are still alive and are mighty cross about your digging up *any* of their grandparents. They don't feel half as scientific about grave robbing as we might."

She sat on a crate as she insisted, "You surely must be joshing, Mr. MacKail. Look at those finely worked flint tools and well-fired potsherds. Then tell me they were buried with the remains of mere Diggers."

He sat down on a nail keg to reply, "You can call me Stuart if I get to call you Nancy. I can see you don't know much about Yana. To begin with, 'mere diggers' is sort of insulting. All the Sierra tribes dug for bulbs and edible roots. But the Yana *are,* not *were,* more advanced by far than the desert tribes to the east. I just heard tell of a white girl who dug bulbs in this same valley. She didn't know as much about digging as your so-called Diggers. I just had supper this afternoon with some Yana. They had compound bows, and they were passing around a pipe with a bowl of well-carved and polished jasper. Those old skin scrapers and carving knives ain't made of flint, by the way. They're chert. Takes a good stone knapper to work chert. The Yana never were and still ain't subhumans grubbing for roots. They're hunter-gatherers, at least as advanced as the eastern woodland tribes, albeit more peaceable when left alone."

She stared at him uncertainly and said, "That's not the way the local Indians have been described to us by the whites up here, Stuart."

To which he replied with a thin smile, "I know what the mining men who stole this valley say about the folks they robbed. It could spoil the taste of a mint julep if it occurred to you that the folks picking your cotton in the hot sun had human feelings. I'd best have a talk with your father in the morning, before he digs up any more dead Diggers. The Yana still knap mighty sharp arrowheads, and they're mighty vexed about his search for a long-lost race that some of 'em still remember fondly."

CHAPTER
FIVE

The saloon was crowded when Stringer got back to it.
The barkeep served him another beer without asking for
company scrip or anything else. Then he must have
mentioned Stringer to someone further down the bar, for
a morose-looking trio of gents closed around him a few
moments later.

The one in the rusty black suit with a mail-order
badge pinned to its lapel said, "I'd be Clem Watson,
town law for Consolidated Minerals. This other gent
here would be my deputy. Young Saunders, with the
Mex hat, would be a county deputy from Quincy. Who
did you say you might be, stranger?"

MacKail put down his beer and said, "I'd be Stringer
MacKail from the *San Francisco Sun*. I hope you'll notice I'm reaching for my wallet with my left hand."

Watson nodded, and Stringer got out his press pass
and I.D. to show them. "I was sent up here to do a

feature on the Great Yana Uprising. I hope it's not a private fight."

"We thought we'd about won until this afternoon," Watson said. "Young Saunders here brung his fellow deputies in full of arrows. We told 'em to let sleeping dogs lie. But did they listen?"

Saunders seemed more interested in Stringer than in Indians as he hovered his gun hand near his tied-down Colt '74 with a heap of thoughts running around in his sly gray eyes. He waited until Stringer was putting his wallet away before he went for his gun.

It wasn't the best move he could have made. Stringer had been hoping he wouldn't. But he'd half expected him to, so he beat the kid to the draw and put three rounds in his chest.

One would have done the job, he saw, as Saunders sprawled at their feet with his own gun half out and a sad little smile on his dead face. Everyone but the two remaining lawmen had taken cover. But as the gunsmoke drifted toward the doorway, Watson and his deputy were still there, with their own guns out. Watson said, "I'd say you just got yourself in one hell of a mess, old son. Give your gun to old Jimbo, and let's talk about it. Do you make a habit of shooting deputy sheriffs?"

Stringer handed his still warm .38 to the one called Jimbo as he answered, "Nope. He wasn't a deputy sheriff. He was fixing to gun me and go on saying he was. That's how come I gunned him first."

Watson said, "I noticed he was slapping leather. You killed him before I could ask him why. Might *you* know, old son?"

Stringer nodded. "Someone's been out to stop me

from getting here since I left the city. That one and his pals weren't out hunting Indians this afternoon. They were after me when some Yana gave 'em a big surprise. Saunders there must have wanted the bounty someone's posted on me. Now you know about as much as I do."

Watson shook his head. "Not hardly. I've known all three of 'em as deputy sheriffs for a good three days or more. They showed me their badges and I.D. the first day they rode in. I never saw you before, and it seems I'd just seen you when you commenced to put bullets in young Saunders. Anyone can flash a fake press pass at an old country boy, you know."

Stringer shrugged. "Anyone can pick up a tin star in a hock shop, too. So we're even on that. Why don't you check us all out? It should only take a few minutes to wire both San Francisco and Plumas County, right?"

Watson brightened. "Good thinking. Why don't we all go over to the telegraph shack together? Jimbo may as well hang on to your gun until we get us some answers to all of this bullshit."

Stringer didn't argue. He knew Watson would simply have shot him by now if he was in on the deal. The three of them went out, and they marched him over to the mining complex. An old watchman with a shotgun fussed at them until he recognized the two town lawmen. Then he unlocked a dark shed for them. Jimbo lit the coal oil lamp over the telegraph key. Stringer noticed old Watson had a pretty good hand as he sat down and commenced to signal for a patch-through to Western Union's long lines.

Stringer could read Morse by ear, so he was rolling a smoke with a relaxed expression when the older lawman finally turned around to say, "Give him his gun back,

Jimbo. He seems to be who he says he is, and Plumas
County says we got sold three goldbricks. They never
sent no deputies to help us, cuss their cold hearts. They
say they got all the pesky Indians they want, and that
it's up to Lassen County or the Army to bail us out."

As Jimbo returned Stringer's .38 he complained,
"Lassen's already told us it was up to the Army, and the
damned Army keeps saying they'll get back to us later."

Stringer put his gun away and lit his smoke before he
told them both, "It just so happens I know some Yana.
One gal who pretended to be a mighty friendly Yana
seems to have been in on the plot to knock me off. But
others might be more reasonable. I could likely get them
to quit pestering you down here if I could tell them your
outfit meant to pull out once it dug all that cinnabar, and
that you'd put a stop to robbing Indian graves around
here."

Watson got out a cigar for himself as he said, "The
company figures no more than a year or so before that
cinnabar vein bottoms out. I have nothing to say about
that professor hunting for extincted redskins. He has a
permit from some college. So far, he ain't bothered nobody in town."

Stringer insisted, "This is an incorporated township,
and you're the law here. Couldn't you pass a local ordi-
nance forbidding the practice? It can't be sanitary, you
know."

Watson bit off the tip of his cigar and spat it on the
floor. "As I hope you just noticed, and lucky for you,
I'm a live-and-let-live cuss. They ain't dug no bones
near anyone's drinking water, and nobody but a few
pesky Diggers seem to mind."

He lit his cigar and got back to his feet as he added,

"That professor has more friends in high places than any fool Digger. If they don't like what he's doing, let 'em bury their dead some other place. I'd as soon peg shots at unwashed redskins as face a lawsuit. The professor would surely commence one if I was to put him out of business with no better reason than a few pissed-off Indians."

Jimbo nodded and said, "Indians are always pissed off about something. The way you deal with an Indian is to shoot him in the head to gain his undivided attention."

As they filed back outside and the night watchman came over to lock up after them, Watson said, "I'd say that was it for tonight. Do you have a place to bunk in town, Stringer?"

MacKail shook his head and went on reloading his S&W. "I was about to ask about that in the saloon when that gunslick threw down on me. I lost my bedroll with my pony, and it does get cold up here after dark."

Watson said, "I don't want you going back to the saloon until we tidy up after your last visit. You can bed down in my hayloft. Jimbo will show you the way, and my old woman will give you some blankets you can use. Now I got to see to planting that dead liar you stuck us with. It don't seem decent to bury him anywhere near poor little Mary-Jo Crocker, but if we do bury him anywhere else that professor will likely dig him up to admire his skull. You boys go on to my place. I'll work something out."

Less than an hour later Stringer was bedded down on clean straw and a blanket that could have used some airing and beating. It smelled of some woman and violet perfume. He wished it didn't. He'd only caught a glimpse of Watson's "old woman," who'd fussed at Jimbo for waking her up and hadn't seemed all that old. But trying to fall asleep alone, all keyed up reminded of womankind with every breath, was a bit of a chore. He was still mighty sore at old Lola, but he still sort of missed her company right now. Thinking about other gals, like that willowy Nancy Gore, didn't do a thing to steady his nerves, and, damn it, there was another woman in bed alone just across the yard from this infernal stable.

He knew better than to dwell on *that*. He considered going back to the saloon and finding out how much beer he still had coming. But he knew that could piss old Watson off too. Smoking in a hayloft could be as dangerous as messing with another man's woman. So he just tried like hell to fall asleep, knowing that that was about as tough a way to do it as there was.

He knew it wasn't as early as it had been, and he'd surely had a hard enough day. He'd hiked all over creation and put himself through more than one good scare since last he'd kissed old Lola and told her he'd be right back. He wondered who was kissing her now and grasshoppered to other, more important considerations, one after the other, as he kept coming up with more questions than answers. Every time he started to relax, one of the ponies in the stalls below seemed to stomp a hoof, as if they knew a man was trying to get some damned sleep around here.

He told himself he ought to feel good about ponies down below to serve as big dumb watchdogs. The mastermind behind all those attempts to slow him down had lost some pawns, but the game wouldn't be over until both sides figured out what they were playing. That brought him wide awake again, of course.

Then he heard more noise down there and heard Watson call out, "Are you sleeping comfortsome, old son?"

To which the only sensible reply could be, "Not now, damn it. What time is it?"

"Pushing eleven," Watson called back. "We got Saunders buried, and the ponies them rascals rode in on to sucker us has been impounded as company property. I was outvoted by the site manager on planting that last rascal. It seemed wrong to me to have three mysterious and sinister strangers buried next to pure little Mary-Jo. But, as it was pointed out by the boss, a settlement this size can't hardly afford more than one burial ground. We picked the one we have because the slope was already clear and the ground was soft digging."

Stringer grimaced in the darkness of the loft and called down, "You picked a bulb field, then. Nice going. The Indians watching from the ridges must love to watch you planting corpses where their women dug up food."

Then he caught himself and shut up before he could give the company man any ideas about oak groves still standing in this half-wrecked valley.

Watson called back, "Well, I mean to plant me for the night now. Jimbo told me my old woman took good care of you. But is there anything else you might want, old son?"

Stringer replied, "Yep, sleep." Which made old Watson chuckle and head for his back door across the yard. Stringer couldn't help wondering wistfully how good that young wife of his would take care of the old coot.

He found out a few minutes later when, over the muffled complaints of a woman, he heard Watson clearly shout, "I told you I was *tired,* damn it!" And then, after some door-slamming and the sound of breaking crockery, it got quiet again.

Stringer waited until he was sure things meant to stay that way. Then he threw aside the top blanket, sat up, and hauled on his boots with an evil grin. As he eased down the ladder and got the gardening tools he recalled from before, he muttered to himself, "You sure are a sneaky little rascal, MacKail."

Finding the burial ground by moonlight turned out to be easier than he'd dared to hope. He'd already figured a good bulb slope had to face south. The whitewashed picket fence they'd enclosed their graveyard in was visible some distance away in the moonlight and would serve to confuse the casual eye about movement on the far side of the ghostly white pickets. He eased through the gateless opening and found four grave markers lined up neatly in the center of the mostly empty plot. He didn't have to risk a match to surmise that the small slate gravestone marked the resting place of the miner's daughter while the slabs of wood marked the graves of the three dead owlhoots. So he just got right to work.

He began by leveling the mound of fresh dirt on the grave of the late young Saunders, fanning the loose soil far and wide in the ankle-deep summer-killed grass with the shovel he'd borrowed. Then he moved to the east of the little girl's grave, at the far end of the line, and used more care as he cut out a six-foot circle of sod. He knew neat square edges attracted the human eye. He pie-wedged the sod into handy totes and used them to make

the place where Saunders lay appear to be undug grass.
Then he simply had to pull up the grave markers and
shift each one grave east. The heavier slate stone of
Mary-Jo got shifted to mark the bare soil—and nothing
more—he'd exposed. Then, having done the easy part,
Stringer took off his hat and jacket, nippy as the night
air was, and proceeded to dig down to nobody. Some of
the bulbs he uncovered near the surface were big and
yummy-looking. He put them in his hat for now.

He didn't have to dig more than a yard or so down,
seeing the soil was so soft and the edges so crumble-
prone. He even raked some of the soil back into the hole
to encourage the view that Indians might dig carelessly.
Then he put his jacket back on, gathered up the rest of
his gear, and headed back to the Watson place, feeling a
mite shitty about the dead child's parents but sort of
pleased with himself nonetheless.

He got rid of the bulbs in the sewer ditch. He put the
shovel and rake back where he'd found them. When he
climbed the ladder back up to the loft, he found he had
company. Watson's young wife whispered, "Where have
you been? I've been waiting here at least an hour."

He could see by the moonlight filtering through a
small grimy window at the far end of the loft that she'd
been waiting long enough to get undressed, too. He
gulped and asked the naked lady reclining on the blankets in the hay to what he owed the honor.

"That old fool hasn't touched me for months," she
said, "and a young woman like myself has needs, damn
it."

Stringer shucked his hat and gun rig, but left everything else right where it was as he told her soberly, "I
know. We all have to eat. Getting married up with a gent

who has a good job may have working for a living beat."

She protested, "I married him fair and square. I like to screw, and he said he needed me. He never said he needed me to cook and sew and play with my poor self whilst he lay slugabed in another damned room. A woman needs a real man to pleasure her, not an old dog who just growls and snores at her. You look like a real man to me. I didn't dare let on in front of Jimbo, but I could see right off that you was young and husky. So what are you waiting for? Don't you think I got a nice body too?"

Stringer sighed and said, "It would be hard not to notice, ma'am. Would it help if I told you I'm tempted as hell?"

She patted the blanket by her bare hip. "Don't just sweet-talk me. I don't need romantical bullshit. I'm already hot as a pistol and ready to give you a ride you'll long remember, cowboy. What are you waiting for? Let's get *to* it!"

He shook his head and said, "I'd sure like to, but I can't. Your man has treated me decent. It would be indecent of me to repay his kindness by messing with his wife."

"Pooh, he treats me as his wife in name only. And he'll never know, will he?"

Stringer said, "We'd know, and however he feels about you and vice versa, you *are* his wife, in name or whatever. I can't say I've never busted that particular commandment, weak-natured as I am. But at least I can say I've never busted it with the wife of a man I owed."

"Can't you do it just this once? I'm just suffering like

anything from pure neglect, and is it my fault I'm wed to a man too old for me?"

"Yep. You could have said no when he asked you to marry him. You could still leave him. You got grounds for divorcing him under California statutes on such matters, if you ain't trying to lead me astray with a mean fib."

She insisted he didn't understand. But he said, "Sure I do. You're not ready to leave his bed and board to make your own living, but you want to screw around on the side. That's not the way your wedding contract reads, ma'am. There's nothing in the fine print saying anything about forsaking all others unless you meet someone you'd like to play slap-and-tickle with. That's one reason I'm still single. I've always felt a contract was a contract, and I just said I have a weak nature."

She lay back and began to bump and grind in the moonlight as she moaned, "Show some of it to *me*, then. Show your weakness hard, and put it in me deep, damn it!"

He already had a pretty good erection inside his jeans: he was human, and she was really built. But he insisted, "You'd best get dressed and back to the house, ma'am. This is just causing the both of us discomfort and chagrin."

She opened her eyes to say in an ominous tone, "If you don't do right by me I'll tell my husband, and he's the *law*."

Stringer blinked and replied, "I noticed. What were you aiming to tell him? That you tried to get me to commit adultery behind his back, on his own property, and that I refused?"

"I can tell him you'd snuck out someplace when I

came out here to make sure you were comfortable. I can tell him you just came back with his digging tools like you'd been out highgrading or whatever. He'll sure ask you lots of questions about that, if you're not nice to me. So how's about it?"

Stringer didn't answer. He had to study on her threat. He knew the sensible way out would be to just give in to her. That way, he'd have more on her than she had on him, and it wasn't as if the poor gal wasn't mighty tempting to begin with. He knew that even if he didn't take her up on her offer for the sake of a good cause, he was surely going to wind up mad as hell at himself some future night when he was alone and hard-up and recalling all the naked ladies he'd ever seen. He started to reach absently for a shirt button. Then he caught himself and said, "You just go and tell your man whatever you want, ma'am. I'm sure he'll understand your reasons for creeping out of the house to me after he was asleep. Tell him I tried to rape you, and then tell him why you didn't call for help, with an armed lawman just across the yard. Then I'll tell him he has a no-good wife, and we shall see what we shall see."

She called him a bastard and likely a fairy as she crawled off across the hay, dragging her nightgown with her bare ass flashing at him in the moonlight.

He waited, but he didn't hear the back door slam as she sneaked into the house, where she belonged. Stringer left his boots on this time, as he covered himself again and tried to relax. It seemed easier now. All that digging on top of all that hiking had left him bone weary all over. He didn't recall falling asleep. He never did. But the next thing he knew he was in this big public library, looking through the racks, and Jack London had plagiarized his story about the Wild Bunch, the bastard. So he got down the book and carried it over to the Gibson Girl behind the library desk, hoping she wouldn't notice he seemed to be naked as a jay. Nobody else in the library seemed to pay any attention to his naked body, even though they all had lots of duds on, and a couple of 'em were roller-skating across the marble floor. Then all hell seemed to be breaking loose outside. So he opened his eyes and woke up.

The first thing he noticed, with pleasure, was that he had his shirt and jeans on after all. Then he saw it was daylight outside and that he had to take a leak. He crawled over to the window and pissed in the dry straw as he peered out to see folks running toward the hillside burial ground. He nodded, got back to his blankets, and quickly slipped into his hat, jacket, and gun rig. Then he dropped down the ladder and joined the general stampede at a more sedate pace, knowing what he'd see up yonder.

As he joined the crowd around the raw hole he'd dug in the dirt to mark with the little girl's headstone, others, bless them, had already trampled all the grass nobody was supposed to be under.

The deputy called Jimbo caught Stringer's eyes in the crowd and confided, "Now they've really gone too far! The son-of-a-bitching Diggers have dug up little Mary-Jo, casket and all!"

Another man chimed in, "Watson's up among the trees, scouting for sign. I sure hope he finds some. Why on earth would Indians want to dig up an innocent child's bones? She never done them no harm."

Stringer shrugged and said, "Mayhaps they're taking

up saltu customs. Haven't you boys been digging up dead Indians who never done *you* harm?"

"That's not the same at all!" Jimbo protested. In the first fool place, none of *us* ever dug any sort of bones up. That doc from the college or whatever is the only one around here interested in Indian graves. In the second place, the doc has scientifical reasons for collecting Indian bones. Them goddamned diggers don't study science stuff, do they?"

"Maybe they figure it must be heap strong medicine, seeing folk digging like gophers down here. Or mayhaps they're just trying to get even. You can see how upset everyone is about little Mary-Jo's missing bones. Perhaps Indians feel the same way about their own dead."

Jimbo swore and snapped, "We'll just see about that. We was having enough trouble with them Indians just digging mercury!"

So Stringer nodded, drifted back, and, having stirred up the hornet's nest, strode off to warn the people who figured to get stung.

At the anthropology camp, he found everyone eating breakfast a mite late, being mostly city folk. Nancy Gore waved him on in and offered him a seat at their long trestle table as she introduced him to her father and his two assistants, a white boy and some sort of breed. Dr. Gore himself was a distinguished-looking gent of about fifty. He had a firm shake and a friendly smile, at first. Stringer allowed he could use some breakfast. But before he touched the coffee or flapjacks served by their camp cook, a fat old Paiute woman in an apron and Mother Hubbard, Stringer felt obliged to announce, "I just came from the graveyard down near the mine. A lot of the townsfolk are upset and may be headed this way. Seems the headstone of a little white gal now marks little more than a hole in the ground."

Dr. Gore stopped smiling. His daughter, Nancy, gasped and said, "That's awful! Who would want to desecrate the grave of a child?"

Stringer dug into his flapjacks as he casually replied, "They seem to feel it was Yana work. They can't even find her casket, let alone her bones. Maybe the Yana want to measure her skull to see if she was superior, inferior, or whatever."

Dr. Gore snapped, "That's ridiculous! The Yana were, in fact, rather advanced. But not *that* advanced. The Diggers up this way now are unrelated to the extinct Yana, by the way. So revenge seems out of the question."

Stringer could see by the self-certain gleam in Gore's eyes that the man just didn't want to hear that the bones he admired and the neighborhood Indians he dismissed as mere primitives could be from one and the same tribe. Stringer washed down a mouthful of food with black coffee and said, "Either way, I'd hold off digging up any more Indian graves for now. I know you have a permit, and I understand your interest, but I'm not sure either the local whites or Indians do right now." He sipped more coffee, which was waking him up just right, before he added, "I was telling your daughter here last night that there's plenty of Indian skulls to study without getting anyone upset."

Dr. Gore shook his own skull and said primly, "Not the people I'm studying. The extinct Yana were a superior race, not at all related to the common tribes of the West Coast. Aside from having bigger brains, they

ground stone tools at the level of the European Neolithic. I've yet to find a stone plowshare, but I'm certain
I shall, if I keep searching. They seem to have reached
the stage where our own ancestors discovered farming,
and that means plowed fields, you see."

Stringer said, "Not hardly. The Aztec and such are
on record as being farmers, where they didn't live in big
cities, but they never used any plows. The Spanish
caught 'em planting corn with digging sticks. You might
say they were Mexican Digger Indians. I hate to be the
one who has to tell you this, sir, but the Yana are not
extinct, and you won't find any plowshares no matter
where you dig around here."

Dr. Gore favored Stringer with a disgusted look and
asked the breed down at the end of the table whether the
Yana were extinct or not. The breed replied, "All gone.
Years ago, before the Gold Rush even. My mother's
people were Shasta. The Shasta tell tales of Yana fighting them in the Shining Times. They once had a big war
over some oak flats. The Yana were all killed and never
came back."

Dr. Gore shot Stringer a triumphant look.

Stringer said, "All right. The Shasta were a big tribe.
They chased some Yana from disputed gathering
grounds. That doesn't mean all the Yana were killed. Is
this a Shasta valley?"

The breed shook his head. "No. The few people
around here are stray Maidu, I think."

To which Stringer replied, in a surer tone, "They're
Yana. You don't have to take my word. At least two
English-speaking Indians I've spoken with recently, told
me they were Yana. You don't have to poke about in
Yana graves to study 'em, Doctor. I could get you some

live Yana to study if you'd be willing to put all those Yana bones back where you found 'em."

Dr. Gore commenced to give him a lecture on lost tribes instead. He'd just gotten wound up when old Watson rode in on a bay, leading a buckskin by it's reins. He dismounted to join them, holding a sheet of yellow foolscap in one hand. He handed it to Dr. Gore, saying, "This just came in for you over our private wire. We keep telling Western Union we ain't a branch of their fool company, but will they listen?"

As Gore read the message, the lawman turned to Stringer and said, "This buckskin is your'n for keeps, since Saunders won't be using it no more. I hope you don't mind the Mex saddle, and you'll note I lashed on a fresh bedroll and canteen lest you catch whatever was ailing him last night. We're riding out after them Diggers. Seeing as you seem to know so much about 'em, we want you to come along."

Stringer nodded and finished his coffee as he rose from the table.

Dr. Gore groaned, "Oh, no!" and told his daughter, "That mule-headed fool, Professor Robbins, is on his way up here with his own expedition." I won't have it! Robbins is no more than a pothunter filled with crackpot theories about Asiatic tribes!"

Watson looked concerned and muttered, "That's just what we need. *Two* bone hunters digging up dead Indians at once!" Then he added, "We don't want you doing that no more, Doc. The site manager says you're not to disturb no more Indian graves until we get to bury the ones as dug up Mary-Jo."

Dr. Gore protested, "I have a permit, damn it!"

Watson replied dryly, "Not from Consolidated Minerals, Doc. It's on our claim you've been digging, and it's on our heads if said digging has caused us more trouble then we already had."

Then he said, "Let's go, Stringer. The boys are waiting for us down at the town corral. It's our fervent hope that you can put us on the trail of them Indians. I hope *you* feel fervent too, for the boys are mighty vexed about little Mary-Jo, and you know how boys feel about strangers when they can't find anyone else to take their anger out on."

Stringer did. So for openers he led the eighteen-man posse to the last place he'd stopped with the treacherous Lola, saying he was backtracking and knowing it was one hell of a ways from that lava tribe and Joe Malliwah et al. It took close to two hours of mighty rough riding, and that served to do wonders for their first enthusiasm. Both the site manager and mine supervisor had tagged along, overweight, in business suits. They sure cussed a lot when Stringer led them through high chaparral, and more than one old boy who was dressed more sensibly bitched about not having chaps on his legs or taps on his stirrups. Stringer got hung up with a branch of sticker-bush through his stirrup now and again, but it didn't feel so bad when a rider knew where he was going. He finally got them to the watered clearing where he'd last seen Lola. He reined in and called out, "Here's where I last saw my pony," and they all dismounted to either scout for sign or flop in the cool ferns.

The deputy called Jimbo was first to notice anything. "Two steel-shod ponies headed west from here at a lope. How come you didn't say you was leading a pack-horse, Stringer?"

MacKail knew how to ask trick questions too. So he

replied, truthfully, "I rode this far aboard a paint. I suspect some fool Indian had to be riding the other."

That inspired Jimbo to explore further to the west in what Stringer sincerely hoped was poison oak. Meanwhile another company hand had found where Stringer's heels had scuffed some dry duff the day before. He called out, "Did you head up this slope one time?"

Stringer replied, "Why should I have?" since he didn't want them tracking that way.

But the hand and a couple of others did, cuss them. So just about the time Jimbo walked back to them, muttering about the damned springy duff holding no more sign than a welcome mat, they all heard a holler from up on the ridge above them and Stringer had no choice but to walk on after them, looking as innocent as he could manage.

CHAPTER
SIX

As Stringer caught up with them around that bay tree he'd been pinned against that other time, Watson pointed up and told him, "You were lucky as hell, Stringer. Look up yonder."

Stringer did. The Yana would have recovered that arrow if it had been at all the kind they fancied. Since it wasn't, it was still stuck deep in the bay bark. Jimbo said soberly, "That's the same kind of arrow them white boys was stuck with when young Saunders brung 'em in to bury."

Watson said, "I noticed. That's why I just told Stringer how lucky he was. The Diggers must have stole his pony whilst he was crapping or whatever down the other way. Then, before they got around to tracking him, they heard Saunders and his pals up this way. We know how *that* turned out. Circle out and scout for more sign, boys."

They did. It was the mine supervisor, bless his fat hide, who found horse apples and a lot of scuffed-up duff down the far slope and yelled about it a lot.

As they all joined him, Watson looked around and said, "This must have been where young Saunders was holding the three ponies. He told me they'd heard something and that his pals had scouted ahead on foot. That was where he found them later full of arrows."

The site manager spied something in a nearby clump of madrone, blinked in surprise, then reached in to haul out that Paiute bow they'd meant to use on Stringer. The site manager laughed like a clever kid and said, "Here's the murder weapon. One of 'em, anyway. One of those Diggers must have dropped it as he ran off, likely wounded."

Watson took the bow and held it high to examine as he said, "It's a Digger bow, sure enough. I remember seeing bows like this as we was crossing the Nevada desert, years ago. Doc Gore must be right about 'em being Paiute, Goshute, or whatever. They got no more right to be up in these mountains than we have, the treacherous trespassing sons of bitches."

Jimbo looked thoughtful. "Saunders never said him and his pals had enjoyed much of a fight with 'em. He told me he'd just waited for his pals an hour or more and then led the ponies on to find 'em dead on the mountain."

Watson shrugged, handed the trophy back to the man who'd found it, and opined, "Saunders told us they were deputy sheriffs as well. His lying pals might have got off a few shots as they went under. There's no way to ask him if he heard any now. The question is which way the rascals run after they stole Stringer's pony and arrowed them other boys."

Jimbo said, "The pony tracks led west, as far as I could follow them."

Stringer, standing west of Jimbo, broke a juniper twig with his fingers, unseen, before he announced, "Someone sure tore past this juniper fast, and to the west as well. Ain't Mount Lassen over that way? And don't the Indians up this way call Lassen the center of their world?"

Watson said he'd never heard that before, but that it made sense. So they all went back down to mount up and ride west, searching for sign and even finding some, they thought, whenever someone noticed where a critter had been at the brush.

In the end it was the site manager who called a halt, observing, "I got both knees bleeding now, and those Diggers have a hell of a lead on us. We don't even know that the same band dug up that white child's casket. I vote we call it a day, boys."

Since all the men but Stringer worked for him, and since Stringer knew they were on a fool's errand for certain, nobody voted against the weary gent. Stringer was tempted to suggest they cut straight over to the wagon trace for easier riding on the way back, but he kept quiet, and, sure enough, Watson brought the motion up and they all agreed they'd busted through more than enough chaparral for the day.

Once they'd made it down to easier riding, Stringer fell in beside the site manager to ask if he had a light. The now ragged boss man give him a match for the smoke he'd just rolled and got out a tailor-made for himself. Stringer waited until they were chatting casually about the woes of mining mercury in such dumb surroundings before he asked, as if just passing the time, how much cinnabar they were jawing about.

The site manager shrugged and said, "No more than a few years' worth, I hope. It's not a very rich vein, and Lord knows mercury is heavy stuff to carry out of these damned mountains. But the stockholders don't have to blast and muck hard rock. They got to sit on their asses and clip coupons while we do all the work. So as long as there's any profit to 'em, we'll likely be stuck up here."

Stringer asked what sort of a profit they were talking about. The site manager replied, "Marginal. The mercury market is down, and you just can't get hard-rock miners to work for nothing. But as long as there's any profit at all, the stockholders will want it. Clipping coupons is a mighty easy chore next to figuring a better place to invest your money. You got to get their stock dividends down to less than the banks will pay as interest before the bastards sit up and take notice. I'm hoping that once the Quicksilver vein bottoms out they'll send me back down to San Diego County. There's still some cinnabar in them coastal hills, and you can get into a real city on weekends."

Stringer agreed the gals in San Diego were pretty, and they jawed about less important matters to him as they rode on back to Quicksilver. They were almost there when the mine superintendent drifted up to join them, bitching about the time they'd have to make up by working late that evening at time-and-a-half.

Stringer kept his mouth shut and his ears open. That gave him a shot at learning a little more without asking nosy questions. He was paid to be nosy, but it made some people proddy, and since he was also paid to know at least a little about a lot of things, he was able to follow most of their mining jargon as he smoked and appeared to admire the hills all around.

He learned that Trevor, the one in charge of digging and refining the mercury, seemed to have as much resentment of authority as his Welsh name called for, while Porter, the site manager and overall boss, was more easygoing as long as he could tell company headquarters things were going as well as anyone could expect in such dismal surroundings. When Trevor said he was hard pressed for pit props down in the shaft, old Porter told him there were still plenty of oak trees in the valley.

Trevor winced like he'd been stung by a bee. "You can't use oak for pit props, look you. The wood is strong, but it doesn't talk to you before it gives. This is earthquake country, and we like at least a few seconds' warning before the mountain sits down on us. Fir props are best, and juniper creaks almost as much before it gives. But my lads have cut all the juniper about the valley, and there was never enough fir to begin with, you see."

Porter looked annoyed. "We'll have to send out some well-armed logging crews, then."

To which Trevor answered, "Then who gets to blast and muck ore in the meantime? My lads are paid to produce mercury, not lumber, look you. We need more men up here if we're to make that one vein pay."

Porter shook his head. "We can't take on a bigger work crew than we already have. I'm already providing for close to three hundred people, counting dependents. Even if you could find me a logging crew of celibate monks I'd still have to pay their wages, and we're operating the company store at a loss as it is. You'll just have to do the best you can with what you have, Trevor."

The mine supervisor snapped, "My lads and I have been doing more than the company has a right to expect from mortal clay, look you. The pit would be dangerous enough with proper timbering, and there's only so much rock we can move in twelve hours. If you'd sign on more men we could use them as a night shift, once they'd cut plenty of juniper for us. We can't carry on as we've been doing if you really want to show a profit."

"I'm only asking you to do the best you can," Porter replied. "This newspaperman and I were just discussing how much nicer mucking mercury would be down near San Diego."

Stringer neither answered nor looked at either of them. He tried to avoid company politics back at the press room of the *Sun*. Such feuding was for women and childish men. He'd never understood the point. But he did know it seemed to go on in any work crew bigger than two. So he sensed there could be more than an honest difference of opinion here. Mercury wasn't toxic as a liquid metal. But it gave off fumes that could addle a man's thinking in time, and, even thinking straight, it would only be natural for the company men who did the hard labor to resent the aboveground management. So the men in and about Quicksilver might not present a solid front to outsiders.

Stringer was pretty sure that Porter wasn't worried about nosy reporters. As site manager, he had the power to run anyone he didn't like clean out of the valley. He'd already forbidden the Gores from messing with any more Indian graves, bless him, and he didn't seem to give that much of a damn about the whole operation.

But Trevor was less cheerful and seemed to feel possessive about his own job. Stringer understood his concern about pit props. He'd done features on hard-rock mines before. Could the fat, feisty Welshman have anything else on his mind?

Stringer couldn't come up with any angle Trevor could be out to hide from the outside world. Old Sam Barca, way down by San Francisco Bay, could read Trevor's production figures just by asking for them at the stock exchange. There was neither a way nor a sensible motive to fudge them. And neither Trevor nor Porter figured to be fired if they couldn't show any profit from this operation. The parent company would just transfer them to some other site, and they both seemed to agree they didn't much care for this one.

Stringer was mulling over everything he'd ever heard about petty company politics, unable to come up with even a dumb point that might inspire a mad mining man to hire at least four and perhaps five dangerous folks at the wages dangerous folks demanded, when they all rode into Quicksilver around noon.

Everyone in town seemed to want to hear about Indians at once. Both Porter and Trevor agreed a lot of them belonged down in the mine. So they said so and made it short and sweet in front of the saloon. Watson told them they'd chased the red rascals at least as far as Mount Lassen, which seemed to cheer most of 'em up. But the mother of little Mary-Jo wailed, "Didn't you get my baby back? I can't stand the notion of her poor bitty bones being passed about by grinning savages."

Jimbo, trying to be helpful, suggested, "Aw, ma'am,

your kid wouldn't have rotted all the way to bones yet. She's only been dead a month."

His well-meant words of cheer inspired the young mother to cover her face with her apron and run off screaming.

Watson shot his deputy a dirty look and growled, "You might have put that more delicate, you uncouth cuss."

Stringer felt like riding after the upset mother to assure her the fool kid's likely stinky little corpse had never been dug up to begin with. But he'd never have played such a trick on anyone if he hadn't been thinking about the feelings of more than one cadaver's kin. So he just dismounted, tethered his mount next to the others in front of the saloon, and tagged along after Trevor, knowing the Welshman wouldn't have left his pony back there if he'd meant to stay down in the mine all that long.

When the mine superintendent noticed he had company, he asked, "Isn't MacKail a Scottish name, look you?"

Stringer replied with a nod, "West Highlands. I don't mind if you call us Scotch. We called ourselves Albanach to begin with, so why pick nits, and what about it?"

Trevor said, "We lads of Cymru are Celts, too, you see. The English have never understood any of us, or tried to."

"You sound like my uncle Don MacKail. He's always said my CrazyAuntIda—one word—has never been able to understand him, or his cows, because she's part English. I sort of noticed you and old Porter were unable to agree on the running of a mercury mine."

Trevor grimaced. "Oh, he means well, you see. But

he's just lost underground. Would you like me to show you about the operation, then?"

Stringer smiled. "I'd be back at the saloon right now if I wasn't interested. I've only seen the edges of the layout in the dark so far."

He was almost sorry he'd said that, by the time the dumpy Trevor finished showing off the whole shebang to him. The mine itself was little more than a hole in the ground, running down at a thirty-degree slant and twisting just enough so they had to use carbide lamps down near the working face. A trio of sweaty workers, stripped to the waist, were drilling the wall of cinnamon toast with two sledges and a star drill.

Trevor glanced down at a nearby open box, half filled with dynamite sticks imbedded in sawdust. Then he gasped and demanded, "What's this, then? You blithering idiots have dynamite enought to blow us out the top of the mountain, just sitting there like your lunch sausages, and the face not ready to blow for hours."

The one holding the star drill soothed, "Take it easy, Taffy. We're meaning to put them sticks in the holes as we drill 'em. You expect us to run in and out of this hole like damned old ants, packing a stick at a time?"

"I do! And the caps carried separate as well! Good God, man, don't you know better than to charge a hole before you've drilled every one? It's a shock that sets dynamite off, you see, and you're swinging nine-pound sledges at that steel in solid rock! I want this dynamite out of here until you're set to blast, and then I want no more down here at one time than the job really calls for."

The one holding the drill protested, "We're almost done here, Taffy."

But Trevor snapped, "You'll be done for good if you don't get that dynamite out of here, look you. I'll not have this pit put at such risk because of your careless lazy ways. Get it out of here this instant. I mean it!"

Stringer nudged the irate mine supervisor and said, "We're going to have to go back up anyway. Let me carry the fool stuff for you. That way you both win." And he picked up the dynamite before Trevor could tell him not to.

The fat fumer followed after him with both lamps, protesting they were spoiling the sweat-soaked workmen back there at the face. When they got back outside, Stringer asked where they kept the stuff when they weren't shattering rock with it. Trevor pointed absently at a nearby sandbagged shed, then he called a company man over and told him to put the dynamite away instead. As Stringer handed the box over, glad to be rid of it, Trevor said, "So much for the pit, such as it is. Shall I show you how we refine the ore, then?"

Stringer nodded, and the supervisor led him along a cinder path, past the telegraph shed, to the big but crudely thrown together smelter.

Stringer noticed that the four men refining the ore all had Welsh surnames. That didn't strike him as mysterious. Uncle Don back home was a sucker for a saddle tramp with a Scotch name, whether they could rope worth a damn or not, and the smelter work had to pay a mite better than busting the ore out of the ground.

Most of the brickwork was just dobe. The boiler plate had of course been hauled in. The operation was so simple that Stringer didn't have to ask many questions. Mercury was molten at room temperature, so they didn't need, or want, to use much heat to roast the

crushed ore. A wood-stoked firebox cooked the cinnabar in an airtight oven big enough to bunk in, with the
fires out and the loading trap open, of course. The mercury boiled out of the rock as a mighty poisonous vapor.
Then it drifted into a sort of giant moonshine still to
cool down and run down through water-cooled coils as
the familiar silvery liquid you could bust out of a ther-
mometer—and did, if you were young and curious
enough.

Stringer stood with them to watch the silvery stuff
fall drop by drop into a steel flask a bit larger than a
milk bottle. He saw there were others nearby, waiting to
be filled or toted out to the freight wagons. He knew
that while a strong man could pack a full flask of mercury on one shoulder, it was just about impossible to
keep on one's feet packing *half* a flask, since even that
much of the infernally heavy liquid metal, sloshing back
and forth inside, hit either end of the flask like a sledge-
hammer.

Knowing the Celtic sense of humor, Stringer was
braced for one of them to coyly suggest such a chore for
a greenhorn to try. But nobody did. Trevor had already
shown he was a serious gent about industrial safety. So,
having seen about all there was to see, they left the
smelter, swung around a massive pile of already roasted
tailings, and headed back to town.

Stringer pointed back over his shoulder with his
thumb and observed, "You sure wind up with a heap of
paler pebbles, once you cook the juice out of it. Have
you considered using some of it for paving? These dirt
roads all around will get muddy as hell betwixt now and
next summer, you know."

Trevor nodded but said, "Spent cinnabar is almost as

hard and sharp-edged as broken glass, look you. Besides that, it's Porter's job to see to such matters. He's welcome to all the tailings he wants. We have more of it further up the slope, you see. Every now and again we have to clear away the pile beside the smelter. It takes up much more room broken up and baked than it ever did in the mountain, look you."

Stringer said he'd noticed. They entered the saloon together and had drinks with Porter, Watson, and a few other company men who didn't seem to have anything better to do. Then Trevor said he meant to go home and change his pants. He warned some gents seated at a table that there'd be fire in the hole before school let out and that he expected them to muck a few tons each before they knocked off for serious drinking. They called him Taffy, too, as he strutted out like a pouter pigeon in his torn pants.

Stringer told the smiling Porter, "I know mining men call Welshmen Taffy, but he does seem to take himself more seriously than the men who work under him seem to."

Porter chuckled fondly. "Nobody could take old Taffy Trevor as seriously as he takes himself. But he's a good old boy, under his bluster. They all know he looks after them like a clucking mother hen. Somebody has to cluck at hard-rock men, you know. Left to themselves they live dangerously."

Stringer said he'd noticed that. He didn't mention the open dynamite being treated so casually. That was Trevor's concern, and Porter had enough on his plate for now.

Stringer finished his beer and left. Nobody seemed to care. He untethered the buckskin and rode it up the valley to the Gores' camp. The older man wasn't there. His daughter, Nancy, said he'd left for the county seat in a huff, albeit aboard a pony, to get an injunction from the courthouse allowing him to dig up all the Indian bones he might want to.

Stringer dismounted, smiling thinly as he told her, "I can see he's a stubborn man. He must not believe in any Yana that ain't dead if he's riding that far through Indian country all alone."

She dimpled and said, "Oh, he took Johnny Conner and Uncle Jake with him. Granny Bear and I are here alone for now, and you're invited for supper, if you like."

He glanced up at the sun, saw he'd missed noon dinner and had a few hours to wait for supper, and said, "I'd be proud to take some grub off your hands later, ma'am. Meanwhile, if your Granny Bear is that Indian cook who served me breakfast, I'd sure drink any coffee she has handy."

The willowy blonde called out, and the old Indian gal stuck her head out of a tent to glare at Stringer while the white lady ordered her in another lingo entirely. When Nancy turned back to Stringer and waved him to the al fresco table set up the same as before, Stringer asked her with a thoughtful frown if she talked that way at home as a rule.

Nancy sat him down, took a seat across from him, and explained. "I know a few words of a lot of dialects. Granny Bear is Paiute. She's been with us for years, but she just can't seem to learn much English. Uncle Jake is Shasta and Dutch, I think. They don't get along too well. Uncle Jake refuses to even say thank you in

Paiute. Even Johnny Conners is willing to be that nice to the dear old woman."

Granny Bear came out to slam tin cups and a coffee-pot down on the planking between them. When Nancy nodded and said, "Toki Wah." Stringer didn't have to ask her what that meant. The old gal shrugged and waddled back out of sight. Stringer could see Uncle Jake's point. The least a fat, ugly old woman could do was smile back when folks were trying to be nice to her.

When he commented on this, sipping coffee that was much nicer than the woman who'd made it, Nancy sighed and said, "Paiute are like that. They've been whipped so sullen, even by other Indians, that they just don't seem to have any smiles left in them."

"Yep. Yana are a lot more cheerful."

Nancy sighed, "Let's not start that again, Stuart. You know very well the Yana are extinct."

Stringer glanced at the sky again. Then he asked, "Would you be fair enough to admit even your father could be wrong if I managed to introduce you to some alive and almost well Yana?"

She laughed. "Are you talking about the Diggers up in the surrounding hills? Thanks a lot! Even if they didn't scalp us, how could you prove they were anything but plain old wandering Diggers?"

"Proving it would be up to you. You just said you speak some Paiute. How about Shasta, Maidu, Miwok, Washo, and such?"

"I know at least a few words in all the Sierra dialects, although Paiute and Washo really belong on the eastern slope. So what?"

"So if you met any Sierra Indians you couldn't

savvy, you'd have to admit they had to be somebody else, wouldn't you?"

"I guess so. But nobody knows how the ancient Yana spoke, Stuart. We only know they existed because other tribes tell legends about them—and, of course, because they left distinctive artifacts for us to dig up."

"Look, Nancy, I can show you Yana using and even making such stuff only a few hours ride from here if you're game to trust me about getting you back with all your hair."

She looked mighty hesitant, and he didn't blame her. But he said, "Of course, if you'd rather just study dead Indians and textbooks for all the answers . . . well, who's ever going to prove you and your stubborn old daddy wrong?"

"All right. Let me gather some notebooks for my saddlebag. But if you get us both killed, Stuart Mac-Kail, I'll never speak to you again."

CHAPTER
SEVEN

Neither of them spotted Joe Malliwah before he wanted them to. They weren't supposed to to. When he finally appeared atop a ridge ahead of them, Nancy observed uncertainly, "That rider up there looks more like a cowboy than an Indian to me."

"Sometimes he acts one way and sometimes the other," Stringer admitted. "Stay here while I ride up and explain you to him."

"You want me to stay here alone and unguarded? What if there are other Indians hidden in the chaparral all about us?"

He smiled at her reassuringly. "I'm pretty sure there are. You won't be unguarded. The Yana will surely stomp any snakes coming at you and your pony. They're more timid then rude."

Then he spurred his own buckskin up through the scrub oak to join Joe on the ridge. As he reined in, the

Indian cowboy said, "I see you've picked up a blond pony and a blond woman since the last time I saw you. Which one gives a man the best ride?"

Stringer told him not to talk dirty and added, "She's just a new convert, I hope. I'm not ready to trust her with the location of that lava tube your friends will be wintering in, but do you reckon you could arrange for her to have supper with some Yana in a safer place?"

Joe said he might be able to, given a sensible reason. So Stringer gave him a terse account of his more recent adventures down in Quicksilver.

Joe grimaced. "You sure have been busy. I savvy how introducing that saltu gal to extinct Indians might improve her manners. But I don't think we ought to tell my more bare-ass kin about her daddy's grave robbing."

Stringer insisted he'd just said that and headed back down the slope to rejoin Nancy while Joe rode the other way to wrangle them an invitation to supper.

Stringer explained the situation to the white girl, leaving out a few things she had no call to fret about, and added, "We may as well dismount and rest our ponies. I can't say where old Joe will be riding, and even when he gets there, some Indians are sort of long-winded."

She hesitated until she saw him get down and tether his pony to a bush with succulent leaves. Then she got down herself. "I wish I shared your trust in Diggers," she said. "So many behave like thieving beggers when they don't throw rocks and run off sneering at you."

Stringer found a better bush to tether her pony to than the scrub oak she'd started to choose before he told her, "For a lady in the Indian-studying business, you sure don't know much about real Indians, no offense. White

tramps who skulk about the edges of a camp or settlement are hardly credits to our race, either. What would
you say if some Indian scientist called a hobo or a horse
thief a typical Caucasian?"

She smiled uncertainly and protested, "It's not the
same. All the poor Indians have been degraded by our
expanding civilization. The Noble Savage was before
my time. They were mopping up the last really wild
Apache while I was still a little girl in pigtails. You
forget I've been on many a field trip with my father
since then. I've yet to see a really wild Indian, even in
so-called Indian country."

He wasn't ready to argue that point yet. They found a
fallen log to sit on, with Stringer keeping his gun facing
out and handy, of course, and as they watched their
ponies browse he asked her to tell him more about that
Professor Robbins her father seemed so upset by.

She said, "Oh, Nat Robbins is a nice enough man, I
guess. He and Father only fuss about scientific methods.
Although, of late, they've gotten pretty vitriolic about
each other's methods in their published papers. Father,
as you know, believes in hard evidence one can weigh
and measure. Old Nat takes the position that linguistic
clues and tribal legends can establish the way various
tribes are, or were, related. Some of his notions seem
rather farfetched to Father. Nat, on the other hand,
claims a potsherd or an arrowhead can't tell you much if
you don't know who might have made it or when."

Stringer nodded. "It reminds me of the Great Dinosaur Feud between Cope and Marsh. They came to
blows about which big lizards ate what, and what they
must have looked like with their hides on. It seems to
me the scientific method would be to use all the data

anyone could find. But then, I'm not a scientist, so I don't have to worry about any pet notions of my own."

He began to roll a smoke as he added thoughtfully, "Cope and Marsh actually sabotaged each other's dinosaur digs, and each accused the other of pegging shots on occasion. Have your father and his rival, Robbins, carried their study of wild Indians to that point?"

She shook her head a bit insistently as she told him, "Good heavens, they're both gentlemen. They used to like each other socially. I fear Father was first to refer to Nat as a young whippersnapper in a paper refuting Nat's claim that the Shoshone and Aztec were both related to the Hopi. Nat's somewhat younger than Father, you see, even though he holds a full professorship in anthropology."

Stringer sealed his cigarette paper with his tongue and said, "Robbins may be right about all those tribes speaking a similar lingo. The Paiute talk something like that, too, according to some article I've read."

She wrinkled her pert nose and told him, "It was probably an article by Nat Robbins, then. Father thinks it's wrong to write scientific articles for popular publications."

Stringer lit his smoke before he asked, "How come? Doesn't the general population have a right to read about Indians? Lord knows enough pure pap has appeared about redskins biting the dust in pulp magazines about a West that never was. I should think a more informed account of real Indians would be good for all of us to read."

She shook her head. "Science is above the heads of most laymen. Even if it weren't, Nat's hasty conclusions strike Father more as an attempt to grab publicity

than an attempt to educate anyone. I like Nat better, but
I have to go along with Father that he tends to make
wild stabs. Every language borrows words from others.
Anyone fluent in both English and Paiute can see their
word for medicine, 'pow-wah,' is simply the English
word 'power' picked up from some early squaw man.''

Stringer took a drag on his smoke and observed
gently, "Few western tribes use the word 'squaw.' It's an
eastern Indian term they sort of resent, having heard it
applied to their women by disrespectful white men. I
think the Yana word for woman would be 'marimee.'''

She turned to him triumphantly to declare, "You just
proved my point! A lot of natives exposed to English
use 'Mary' as the word for a wife. Or perhaps it derives
from 'marry me'!"

He shrugged and said, "You'll get a chance to ask
before sundown. I see old Joe Malliwah is back. He
once told me his name means 'wolf,' by the way. I'd
love to hear you twist 'wolf' or, heck, 'lobo,' into
'Malliwah.'''

She couldn't. They mounted their ponies and rode up
to join Joe on the ridge. Nancy seemed surprised when
Joe held out a big brown hand to her and said, "Howdy,
ma'am. You're just in time for supper."

But it wasn't quite that simple. Joe led them high and
low through woods and chaparral, until even Stringer
was having a hard time figuring out just where they
might be. Finally they wound up in a small mountain
meadow in front of a summer lodge the Yana had obviously tossed fresh branches on top of in their honor.

They got down and ducked inside. Nancy was obviously ill at ease at first. But she knew enough to act
polite, and as the old Yana men and women inside, with

no kids to get in the way, warmed up to her attempts to talk to them in Paiute, she began to look more relaxed and confused at the same time.

With Joe translating, she asked if it was all right for her to take notes. The grave old chief Stringer had met before said he'd just love to see some saltu medicine. So Nancy wrote down that *majapah*—their word for "chief"—likely derived from Major Poppa, and she said so to Stringer.

But once they'd been served some acorn mush and deer stew, with implements and in basket saucers that didn't sound at all like any lingo she knew, Nancy began to agree grudgingly that whatever these folk were, they couldn't be members of any tribe she was familiar with.

She knew enough about Indians in general to accept seconds and act as if she enjoyed their cooking. It couldn't have been too tough for her. The Yana had gone out of their way to provide a decent meal, and she said so, sincerely.

Then, as the men smoked, Nancy commenced to compile a shorthand glossary of Yana words by pointing at things and getting the Yana to giggle at her. When the old majapah and an old woman called the same bone spoon different names, she turned to Joe for help.

The cowboy explained, "When Yana are little, living with their mommas in the family wowi—this here is a wowi—they talk woman-talk. Once a boy's been initiated into the watah-gurwah, or men's clubhouse, he learns new words for everything, so he can talk man-talk. It sounds complicated unless you're used to it. But everyone knows both words for everything, in case someone gets drunk and mixed up. Sometimes a man calls something by its woman-name as a joke. Some such jokes can get sort of dirty. So let's say no more about it, ma'am."

She wrote that down and exclaimed, "Heavens, the Slavic languages of the Old World do much the same thing. Men and women speaking, say, Russian use different grammar."

Joe raised an eyebrow. "Are you saying my kin speak Russian, ma'am?"

Nancy laughed. "No. But both languages may well have picked the odd construction up from some Asiatic race long ago. Other Indo-European languages have less confusing grammars than Slavic, and it's no secret the American Indian once lived in Siberia."

She turned to Stringer to add, "Nat Robbins says he can relate most Indian dialects to no more than a handful of Siberian ancestral tongues. He'd have a field day if he could work with these people! I confess that all I can work out is that they share many words with Shasta, some with Maidu, and some with no dialect I know anything about."

Stringer suggested that in that case she'd best take down some more. So she did, nodding with understanding when the word for something sounded familiar and grinning like a kid on Christmas morning when she found a word entirely unexpected. Then she spotted a stone meat chopper one old Yana lady was almost sitting on and asked if she could take a closer look at it. The Yana woman handed it over with a curious look, since to her it was simply what she'd used to cut up some deer meat, and they all looked surprised when Nancy held it up to the light and exclaimed, "We've found flintwork just like this down by Quicksilver in prehistoric burials."

Stringer said, "No you haven't. I tried to tell you and your father the Yana only moved in here a generation or so back. They used to live over on the far side of Mount Lassen. Ain't that right, Joe?"

The English-speaking Indian nodded. "Hoksah. There was too much gold over that way for our people to live in peace. I sure wish they hadn't found that damned mercury. How were we supposed to know what that paint-rock was good for to you saltu?"

Nancy asked to be shown more local stonework. The Indians were willing to indulge her, although they found her enthusiasm for their hardware sort of confusing. She waved a stone-headed wood ax around in an almost threatening manner and proclaimed it a Neolithic war celt.

Stringer glanced at Joe, who told the white girl, "No it's not. It's a plain old woman's hatchet."

She protested that it still struck her as a prime example of Neolithic stone polishing. The old majapah asked Joe what all the fuss was about, and when Joe translated, their host spoke first to an old Yana woman and then said Nancy could have the fool thing if she admired it that much.

Not to be outdone, the other women proceeded to fill a basket with other stoneware, some flaked and some polished smooth. A people who depended on stone for most of their tools weren't all that picky about how they made them. Nancy was of course delighted, and lady enough to ask Joe what they wanted in return.

Joe said, "They don't want anything. Them's gifts, not swaps. But if you want 'em to remember you fondly, that big red kerchief around your neck would do nicely. Hand it to the old man. He'll work it out with his wives."

As Nancy untied her kerchief she asked if all the old women there were married to that one old man.

Joe shook his head and said, "Two of 'em are widowed sisters. It ain't easy, being a majapah. You're expected to marry all the gals nobody else in the band is up to feeding."

Nancy said that reminded her of other misunderstood notions about tribal people and handed the printed calico kerchief to the majapah, who protested it was too great a gift but kept it anyway. Then there was an awkward silence.

Stringer, seated nearest to the doorway, glanced outside and told Nancy, "It's getting on toward sunset. If they wanted us to spend the night they'd have brought more blankets. Are you about ready to head for town now?"

She sighed. "I suppose we should be getting back. But there's so much for me to learn here. I've barely taken down four pages of their words, and I want to know so much more about them. Do you suppose they'd let us come back another day?"

"Depends on how they feel about you. Can we promise 'em their dead will be left in peace from now on?"

She started to nod. Then she said, "I can't speak for Father, but I'm sure that when he gets back he'll be very impressed by this basket of modern stonework that's just like what we've been digging up. I wonder if any of these people would sit still for having their skull shapes measured."

Stringer laughed. "I'd wait until I got to know 'em a

mite better. But making friends with 'em instead of ril-ing 'em sounds like a good start. Meanwhile, let's see if we can get you home before dark. You coming a ways, Joe?"

The cowboy said, "No. You know the way. I have to help these people carry stuff home to their winter camp. They only gave you half a ton of their stuff."

Stringer picked up the basket, which weighed more like thirty pounds, and led Nancy back out to their ponies. He tied her specimens to the bare-wood tree of his Mex saddle while she put her notes away. Then they mounted up in the late-afternoon light to ride back the way they'd come. Nobody came out to wave them off.

As they rode for Quicksilver in the gloaming light, Stringer got turned around more than once. But since he could tell north from south and downhill from up, he figured they had to be about halfway there by the time Nancy was wishing on the first star winking down from a lavender sky.

They found—or stumbled upon—a trail that seemed to be headed the right way. Nancy rode forward to ride stirrup to stirrup with him. He didn't mind that at all. But they'd only traveled that way a short while before Stringer heard a sinister whirring and stiff-armed the blonde off the far side of her pony as the arrow meant for her back grazed his sleeve to go on and thunk into an oak limb just ahead.

Nancy wound up bawling most unladylike curses in a clump of poison oak on her side of the trail. Stringer had rolled off into deep ferns. The two ponies simply kept going, fast.

The cover was better where he was. But Stringer crawled over to the girl, hauled her out of the poison oak, and got them both behind a mossy fallen log, his own .38 drawn as he peered in vain for something to aim it at. He couldn't see more than a few yards into the poorly illuminated greenery all around them.

Nancy sobbed, "Oh, whatever could have made those Yana turn on us?"

"They didn't. That wasn't a Yana arrow. It wasn't aimed so hot, either. I think they were supposed to get me with it."

She protested, "I thought you said those cowboys playing Indian with you were all dead." Then she glanced over her shoulder at the arrow imbedded in the oak bark to add, "Hmm, that does look like a Paiute arrow."

He nodded, "Save for your old cook, there ain't supposed to be many Paiute on this slope of the Sierra."

She swallowed and asked, "What are we ever to do? We've lost our mounts. We only have that one gun of yours to hold them off with, and it will soon be dark."

"I noticed. Since they want to play cowboys and Indians, I'd best go along with their fool game. Stay put. I'm not going far."

He didn't. He just moved off to their right a few yards and fired three rounds straight up. Then he crab-crawled back to Nancy as leaves fluttered down and fusillade of gunshots peppered where he'd just been.

As he reloaded next to Nancy, she asked him why on earth he'd done that. He explained, "They were trying to kill us quiet. I didn't want to go along with that notion. Now just hush up and listen sharp."

They did, but it stayed breathlessly still all around them as the forest kept getting darker. Then, a million years later, the familiar voice of good old Joe Malliwah called out, "Hey, Stringer?"

"Don't answer!" Nancy begged. "What if he's in on it?"

"I'd be mighty surprised. I wouldn't be here if Joe himself hadn't sent for me. I fired that three-shot distress signal with an old Army man like Joe in mind."

Then he called out, "We're over here, Joe. Can I take it you and your kin are the only ones still about?"

The Indian cowboy called back, "You can now. Sign reads two men on steel-shod ponies, leaving in too much of a hurry for our Yana infantry to head off afoot. We recovered your mounts for you, though. They stopped off for some manzanita just a quarter mile downslope."

Stringer got up and helped Nancy to her feet as Joe approached them on his own scrub pony, leading the buckskin and Nancy's bay. As Stringer helped the girl remount, he told Joe, "They were out to pin more trouble on your kin by pinning me, at least, with yet another arrow."

Joe nodded at the now almost invisible arrow imbedded in the nearby limb and said, "We found the murder weapon one of them mean-hearted saltu tossed away. Looks like Shasta workmanship. Not too new. One of the feather vanes on that Paiute arrow is missing. Sinew glue is like that once it dries out. I'd say some sneak has been at a museum or private collection of mixed hunting gear, made at different times by different nations."

Stringer forked aboard his own mount as he opined, "The mastermind must have a lot of old Indian gear to spare if they can afford to get rid of the evidence so freely before riding back to town."

Joe asked, "How do you know they're working out of Quicksilver? Why not a hideout somewhere in these hills? *My* people find it easy to hide out up here, you know."

Stringer shook his head. "If they had a secret stronghold they wouldn't have to keep throwing those bows away. Quicksilver is the only settlement for miles. I'm pretty sure the town law is being run on the level. So nobody would want to return from, say, a quail hunt waving an Indian bow about. Riding out, it would be easier. Nobody pays much attention to anyone riding out because they don't expect them to, see?"

Nancy repressed a shudder. "If what you say is true, those men who just attacked us will be in town as we ride in, and we don't know who they are."

Stringer nodded. "That's why you're not about to live in that canvas tent, guarded by one old Paiute cook, before your menfolk get back from the county seat." He turned to Joe. "It looks like your Yana kin will be having a houseguest overnight. Do you want to talk it over with 'em alone?"

Jo said he'd better and suggested they meet him later at that same now-deserted wowi. Then he clucked to his own pony and did a vanishing act without asking Stringer if he thought he'd be able to find the place in the dark.

Stringer could, but it wasn't easy. As he helped Nancy down again he felt sticky poison-oak sap clinging to her britches. He tethered their ponies and led her inside the dark wowi. He struck a match and got a small fire going. Then he began to rummage along the brush walls as she protested she wasn't cold and that the smoke hurt her eyes.

Stringer said, "You'll have more than itchy eyes
come morning unless I find something to rub you down
with. I happen to be immune to poison oak, which is
just as well, when you consider the hills I grew up in.
But not everyone is, and the Yana spend a good deal of
time hiding in the stuff. So they carry lots of herbs
about with 'em."

She blinked at him and asked, "Are you suggesting I
let you rub herbs all over my naked flesh, sir?"

He chuckled. "You could do it as well yourself, in
the dark, and likely get us both in less trouble."

But he was still searching in vain when Joe Malliwah
and a couple of Yana women joined them at last.

Joe said, "The majapah is afraid to let a strange saltu
woman know where his winter camp is, but he sends
these girls with good blankets and food to make you
both comfortable here for the night. Why are you sniff-
ing like a dog on your hands and knees, Stringer?"

Stringer explained about Nancy rolling in poison
oak. As the Yana women hauled in the baskets and
blankets of woven rabbit skins, Joe explained the problem to them in their own tongue. They both seemed to
think it was pretty funny. But the older one produced a
bundle of wilted weeds and handed it to Nancy.

Joe told her, "This stuff is better than jewelweed. I
don't know what to call it in English. You have to rub it
all over yourself and on your clothes before you put
them back on. It's a good thing you don't have a toothache. Our medicine doesn't do much for that. It's a
good thing we don't eat many sweets."

Nancy looked embarrassed.

Stringer told her, "Don't worry. Joe and I were just

leaving. By the time we get back you ought to be asleep as well as cured."

She wailed after them, demanding to know where on earth they were going. But Stringer didn't like to lie, and the less she knew, the better.

Joe waited until they were mounted up before he said, "I'm with you. But what's the plan?"

Stringer said, "Some son of a bitch wants to play cowboys and Indians. So let's show him how the game can be played, damn it."

They left their ponies hidden a mile outside the mining town and moved in the rest of the way on foot. Most of the mining men and their dependents had turned in for the night by now, so they only had to avoid the lights around the saloon. By this time Joe understood Stringer's plans, even though he didn't care for them and kept saying Stringer was crazy.

They infiltrated the crude industrial complex around the mercury mine's adit. Stringer didn't trust the powerfully built Indian to just knock the old night watchman out without busting his skull. So they fanned out, and when Joe called to the old man and got him to come out of his shed, Stringer was the one who smacked him with a sand-filled sock from his saddlebag. As Joe caught the old watchman's falling form he grunted, "Hear me, I think he saw my face."

"*Bueno*. He'll recall seeing an Indian just before the lights went out. Let's get him over on the far side of the tailings heap, where he'll be safer."

They did, leaving the watchman's shotgun where it lay by the smelter doorway. As soon as they had the old man bedded down, Stringer told Joe, "I can handle the next part here alone. You run up to the far end and go into your Sioux war dance. I'll be waiting to hear some war whoops before I raise hell on my own."

Joe grumbled, "Damn it, I don't know how to do war whoops. I come from a *quiet* breed of redskin."

Stringer insisted, "If I wanted total silence I'd never have asked you to tag along. Just pretend you once rode in Buffalo Bill's tent show. Half his wild Indians are white boys to begin with. You don't have to sound authentic, just noisy, see?"

Joe grinned wickedly and faded away in the darkness. Stringer moved to the dynamite shed, pried the padlock hasp from the wood with his pocket knife, and ducked in to get to work.

He only had to cap and fuse one stick in each box he helped himself to. He lit no fuses until, way off in the distance, he heard Joe empty his six-gun at the stars and yodel like a Comanche with an awesome bellyache.

That caused a heap of windows to light up indeed while the night owls from the saloon boiled out into the street to shout dumb things like, "Circle the wagons! Save your last two rounds for your woman and yourself!"

By this time Stringer had lit his fuses and was headed for the hills at a dead run. He crashed into a wheelbarrow some fool had left in a mighty dumb place. As he sprang back up he heard someone shout, "They're down thataways, too!"

But he was out of range as wild shots commenced to search for his galloping hind end, and then the dynamite started to go off behind him, each thunderous explosion outlining his shadow ahead of him in sullen orange light. By now he was too far upslope to be made out as more than a running figure winking on and off, but make him out someone did.

"Keep you heads down, boys!" the man shouted. "They're around us on every damned slope!"

So the victims of Stringer's prank took cover and would only learn, after a long sleepless night, that the mine adit had been blasted shut and the smelter had been blasted just about flat by Indians, according to the old watchman, once he managed to stagger out of the ruins.

Back on the ridge where they'd left their ponies, Joe said, "That was fun, But hear me, I thought the reason you came up here was to make them stop blaming bad things on my Yana kin."

As they mounted to ride off, Stringer explained, "I wasn't getting anywhere just talking. Most of those miners sincerely believe they've been having Indian trouble. Partly because some of 'em know they should feel shitty about the way they've been raised to treat inconvenient Indians, but mostly because some sneaky bastard has been encouraging the myth with sneaky tricks. I told you neither the BIA nor the War Department thought there could be enough Indians around here to worry that much about."

Joe frowned thoughtfully. "They're liable to take my kin more seriously now. But why did we just help the mastermind sell his story to the outside world? I thought he wasn't on our side, damn it."

Stringer nodded grimly. "He's only on his own side. If I understood his motives I'd have a better notion who he might be. But you have to eat the apple a bite at a time, Joe. I know the old majapah won't like it, but once the BIA has him and his band on their books they'll be a heap better off. It's just too late in the game for any leftover bands to go on trying to live wild. They need an agent to stand up for them. You saw how they were treated when nobody felt they needed a hunting license to treat 'em like wild vermin."

Joe sighed and said, "If they were vermin, at least they were still free. My own band used to roam free. Hear me, I know what happens next. The BIA will want to issue them rations and make their children learn to read and write. Most of them will go along with it. My band did. The saltu ways are tempting. The women will get too lazy to leach acorn meal, once they learn to use white flour. Nobody on my reservation makes those rabbit-skin robes anymore. Wool blankets are too easy to buy, and that weaving was a lot of work. In just a few years the old ways will be gone for these Yana forever. The young men will wear jeans and punch cows, like me."

Stringer grimaced. "You know you had a swell time with the Rough Riders down in Cuba, Joe. That's the way history moves. Someday your grandchildren will look back on your cowboy occupation as a Shining Time. Such times just don't last all that long for anybody."

Joe scowled. "Hear me, you are full of shit. Before you saltu came, my people lived wild and free as soaring eagles. They had a good life. Nobody ever bothered them."

Stringer shook his head. "Bullshit yourself. The life they led tended to be short as well as free. There was more to eat out this way, but some tribes were already fighting over the best acorn groves. Oaks grow slower than populations. My own folks had a Shining Time, to

hear old Scotch drunks moan about it. In the old country
they got to play sad pipe music and have jolly clan bat-
tles until overpopulation and a primitive way of farming
got them fighting more seriously over cows and oats for
their hungry kids. Had we stayed as we were we'd have
likely grown mighty miserable by now. But we were
forced to change, and we did. So my grandfather wound
up an American cattle baron instead of the barefoot
Highland crofter he kept saying he could have been if it
hadn't been spoiled for him by the infernal English,
and, hell, I got to go to Stanford and learn to play a
typewriter instead of a bagpipe. So do you hear me
bitching?"

Joe insisted, "It's not the same. You saltu never knew
what it was like to live really close to nature."

Stringer sighed and said, "I wish you noble savages
would pay attention. How do you think white cavemen
lived? If they'd been having so much fun at it they'd
never have bothered to invent civilization. It took us a
hell of a long time, Joe. You and your folk don't have
near as much work cut out for you, and spare me the sad
details of the fun we've stolen from you. I notice you
light your smokes with matches instead of twirling a fire
stick an hour or so. You'd be walking instead of riding
right now if white men hadn't brought the horse to this
continent. I'll allow there was a time, a mighty short
time, when the Indian had things swell, roaming still
empty range aboard a white man's pony after buffalo
he'd never been able to hunt on foot. But we live in a
world that keeps changing, Joe. Instead of mooning
about the fun your grandmother had chawing her man's
moccasins to keep 'em soft you ought to study on your

granddaughter being a moving picture star or, hell, a ballerina, since you folk like to dance so much."

Joe laughed despite himself. "You've made your point. I can't see these Yana kin of mine toe-dancing, but an Indian agent might be able to keep them alive, whether they like it or not. How do we keep the Army from slaughtering them in the meantime?"

"Hell, the Army has enough trouble tracking Indians that are *really* on the warpath. How are they going to find a band that's only minding its own business in the tanglewoods? The old majapah is about to go into winter quarters. Soldiers just hate searching for footprints in stirrup-deep snow. So they won't go far up in these hills, and in the meantime, I'll have a talk with some decent officers and BIA agents I know."

They were far enough from Quicksilver now for him to begin to build a smoke as he continued, "My real problem is the mastermind who stirred up all this trouble to begin with. I doubt the Army will even scout for Indians if I can tell them who's behind all this nonsense."

"Don't light that yet," Joe said. "We don't know how many fake Indians your mastermind has working for him. Any at all must be costing him much money. What do you think he's really after?"

"Me, for one thing," Stringer said. "After that it gets harder to figure. There has to be something he doesn't want me to write up for my paper. It can't be that there's a mining town or even a band of Yana in these parts. He's guarding some other secret, and for God's sake don't ask me what his secret might be. For if I knew it, I'd know who he was, damn it."

CHAPTER
EIGHT

They split up near the wowi they'd left Nancy in for the night. There was half the night left when Stringer ducked in to see how the white girl was doing. The two Yana women seated by the ruby coals of the central fire nodded at him, said something he couldn't savvy, and left, giggling at one another.

Nancy lay asleep, or half asleep, wrapped up in rabbit-skin blankets. She'd undressed for bed, judging from one bare shoulder exposed to the fire's glow. Stringer glanced about for any bedcovers they might have left for him. There didn't seem to be any. He now understood what they'd been giggling about. There was no way to tell them now that the naked white girl under all that rabbit fuzz wasn't that total a pal of his.

Stringer went back out and got the bedroll from his saddle. He was spreading it out near Nancy when she opened one eye, gasped, and said, "Oh, it's you. I've been so worried. Where have you been all this time?"

"Scouting. Go back to sleep. It's not all that late. But we may have a long day ahead of us."

"I've been trying to. I smell like a drugstore, and these rabbit skins smell just awful. Do you think there could be fleas in them?"

"I doubt it. Indians are more likely to have lice than fleas. Those herbs they rubbed you down with are likely to discourage 'em."

He finished putting his own bedding together and commenced to get undressed. There wasn't much light, and he figured if he kept his back to her she might not notice anything important. But she murmured, "Good heavens, do you think it's proper for us to spend the night like this together, alone and naked?"

He muttered, facing the other way, "You can put your duds back on if you want to. I won't peek. Who do you reckon we'll have to answer to, about what?"

She replied, "Well, I know it's not as if we were in the same bed with all our clothes off. But I fear that if anyone ever found out they'd still assume we'd been sort of naughty."

He flopped down and drew the top blanket over his bare chest as he chuckled and said, "Yep, ain't it hell to have the name and not the game? I've oft considered that about a gal who boards in the same rooming house, down by the bay. Her door gives her a quick beeline up the stairs to mine, and she wanders the halls so casual that I'm sure the other boarders think we're lovers. I've wondered more than once why I bother acting so pure with her, since nobody seems to think I have been."

Nancy wanted to hear more about the gal on the second landing. So he told her tersely about the fool flirt.

Nancy decided, "You're right. No doubt all the others think you've been carrying on an affair with her, and I'd say she had one in mind. The poor thing must be awfully ugly."

He shook his head. "As a matter of fact she's an artist's model and has the shape to prove it. Some times I think I must be a fool myself. But you know what they say about messing around where you work or eat."

She sighed. "Only too well. The scientific world is small and prone to gossip. But what if you and that artist's model managed to be, well, very discreet when you were out of public view together?"

"We'd best drop the subject, lest she owe you a debt of gratitude as soon as I get back to the city. I'm not sure I could trust such a sassy gal to be discreet in any case. No offense, but you gals can be as bad as us men when it comes to playing kiss-and-tell."

She protested, "Speak for yourself. I'll have you know my father still thinks I'm a shy little virgin. I *never* talk about *my*, ah, romances."

He moaned and pleaded, "Why me, Lord? Why do gals insist on telling a man about all the other men who've used and abused them until he commences to feel left out?"

Nancy laughed. "I never asked you to spread that bedroll over there, you know."

He blinked, started to tell her not to be such an infernal tease, then wondered why anyone with a lick of sense would want to say a thing like that and threw off his blanket to crawl her way instead.

There was just enough ruby light for her to see what

he was armed with as he started to get under the rabbit fur with her. She gasped and said, "Wait, I'm not sure I meant that the way you seem to have taken it!"

Then he tossed the top robe aside to expose her smooth bare torso, and she was taking all he had to offer while he kissed her hard to keep her from making any more silly remarks.

From the way she moved her athletic horsewoman's hips in time with his thrusts he assumed she had no more to make. But as they came up for air she protested, "Oh, my God, you're ... going all the way with me, you brute!"

He asked her if she wanted him to stop. She wrapped her legs around him, protesting it was too late to stop now. This was just as well for both of them, since no man born of mortal woman could have stopped just then.

When they climaxed and finally had to stop, at least for a moment, Nancy sobbed, "This is awful. I can't blame you. I know I brought it on myself by speaking so freely, but don't you agree you've behaved just terribly? And, oh, what are we ever to do now?"

He didn't answer. As he began to move in her some more she gasped and pleaded, "Oh, don't! You musn't take advantage of my weakness again and ... and ... if you stop now I'll kill you!"

So he didn't, and by the time he'd persuaded her to try it dog style on her hands and knees she was laughing as she told him how shocked she was by his, and her, animal nature. By the time she got on top to take control of the situation she seemed to feel they were old pals who didn't need to apologize to one another for behaving so pleasantly wild. As she climaxed and fell down against him to crush her perky breasts to his bare chest, Nancy admitted, "This is wonderful. I have to confess I really needed some. Father is such an old fuss, and that silly Johnny never even looks at me."

He asked what about Uncle Jake. She told him not to be a brute, adding, "A girl has to draw the line somewhere. You promise you won't tell anyone about this, not even your Indian cowboy?"

He hugged her closer and said soothingly, "Let old Joe get his own gals. Knowing him, he's likely got one about now."

She giggled and asked if Indians did this the way white folk did.

He said, "Hell, old pard, there's only so many positions anyone can get into."

She replied with another giggle. "I know. I once filched a copy of *Justine* from the restricted stacks at the university. De Sade didn't know what he was talking about. Half of his suggestions hurt, and we couldn't even manage most of the positions."

He didn't ask who'd helped her with the experiments. He didn't want to know. But that did lead them into trying some mighty wild positions as the night went on, including some he'd never even heard of before.

They enjoyed—or at least ate—a hearty breakfast of acorn meal and elk jerky. Then they came upon a secluded mountain tarn on their way back to town, and Nancy said she felt itchy for whatever reason. So they enjoyed an early-morning dip al fresco. Then Stringer examined Nancy's creamy skin for any sign of poison ivy, noticed she looked even blonder all over by broad day, and that of course led to some fun in the ferns

before even she agreed they really ought to get back into
Quicksilver before they were missed.

But they had been already. So when they were spotted topping a rise a lot closer to town a member of the
patrol fired a shot in the air to attract their attention, and
they all met up in the draw between.

Old Clem Watson was in command, of course, with
Porter, the site manager, and a dozen other riders
Stringer only knew to nod at. Watson said Jimbo was
leading another patrol, and that Trevor and some mighty
annoyed hard-rock men were with him.

Watson said, "You two missed a heap of excitement
last night. I take it you was up here together alone overnight?"

Stringer replied, "No. We were surrounded by Indians." While Nancy just went on looking as if butter
wouldn't melt in her mouth. Stringer saw he might have
raised more questions than he'd just answered. So he
added, "We rode out yesterday afternoon to study Indians, Miss Gore here being in the Indian-studying business. We met a handful who seemed friendly enough.
But on the way back someone more hostile pegged at
least one arrow at us. So we thought it best to hole up
until daybreak, and you have my word that neither of us
got much sleep last night."

Watson replied, "I didn't neither. They hit us harder.
This time it was a full-scale raid. They got into the dynamite down by the smelter and commenced to blow
things to smithereens, including the smelter. Caved in
the mine, too. The only thing left to thank the Lord for
was that the savages didn't know which of the buildings
in town might or might not be occupied."

Another rider volunteered, "We got one damned Digger for sure and likely winged at least a dozen more as they run off whooping and shooting back."

While Stringer was still digesting this, Porter shot a wary look around the higher ridges to either side and said, "I'd say we ought to head back while we're still one-up on them, boys. With Miss Nancy and Stringer accounted for, nobody from Quicksilver seems to be lost, strayed, or stolen."

Nobody argued with the man who paid their wages. But Porter was gracious enough to let old Watson remain in the lead as he fell back to guard or perhaps flirt with Nancy. This left Stringer riding closer to Watson. He wasn't sure he ought to be. On the other hand, he didn't want to seem too possessive of the lady he'd just possessed, unchaperoned, now that so many others could peek.

He tried to keep track of what Nancy was saying to Porter back there. It would have been easier if old Watson wasn't jawing at him about things he already knew about. Having set off the blasts himself, Stringer hardly needed to be told how slick the charges had been placed. So he listened with half an ear as he tried to think how Nancy could slip up. It was safe to assume she wasn't telling Porter she liked to get on top, and when you got right down to it, she had no way of knowing about Stringer's other sins of the evening.

The second time Watson bragged about Indian casualties, the man who didn't see how there could have been any raised an eyebrow and listened tighter. Watson was saying, "Diggers have no shame. The young squaw they brung along on the raid was sort of pretty before a lucky shot blowed one side of her skull off."

Stringer frowned and replied, "I never heard of a gal

going along on a raid. You're sure they nailed a *woman?*"

Watson spat and said, "Of course it was a woman. Did you think we was all blind? I know some Digger men wears their hair long and braided, but she was naked as a jay when we found her on the slope by the dawn's early light. Can't say which of the boys got her. Everyone was shooting considerable. It was my own grand notion to put her on ice so's we can show her to the county coroner if and when he ever gets here. The infernal county seems to think we've been joshing them about wild Indians. This time we got us a specimen to show 'em, along with all that wreckage they left in their wake."

Stringer asked cautiously, "I take it they didn't blow up the telegraph shed, then?"

"Oh, they blowed the shed off its foundations," Watson replied. "But wire bends, and the set stayed screwed to the table. We ought to have us a sheriff's posse and at least a troop of cavalry up here anytime now. That'll learn them infernal Diggers."

Stringer didn't answer. He began to build a smoke to give himself time to think. Watson said no more about the raid as they rode on a spell. Then the old man suddenly blurted, "I'm glad you was up here in the hills with another gal last night. For I fear I spited you some, in my thoughts at least, earlier."

Stringer sealed the straw-colored paper with his tongue before he replied, "Oh? How many gals might you have figured I was with at one time, Clem?"

Watson looked away but didn't really surprise Stringer when he said, "Last night I was sleeping when the Indians commenced to blow things up. I run into my old woman's room to guard her with my life, and well, she wasn't there."

"She likely ran outside to watch the fireworks with everyone else."

"That's what she told me an hour later, when we finally met up. I reckon you think I was a fool to marry up with such a young and, ah, restless woman, right?"

"Wrong. I've learned never to advise other men on war or marriage," Stringer said. "Suffice it to say you ought to be ashamed of yourself for suspecting me of adultery, pard."

Watson shot a thoughtful glance back at Nancy and sighed. "Well, it ain't adultery unless one or the other happens to be married. If I ever find out who she *was*, ah, watching fireworks with, I'll blow his fucking head off. I may be getting old, but a man has *rights*, damn it."

Stringer lit his smoke and murmured, "I'd go easy on such talk, Clem. You don't want the whole town talking about it."

Watson grimaced and grumbled, "They likely are, and laughing at me already. They say the husband is always the last to know. You already knew, didn't you?"

Stringer took a thoughtful drag of Bull Durham before he asked the old man quietly where he'd come up with that notion.

Watson said, "She told me over breakfast that you'd been up to something sneaky that first night you stayed in our hayloft. I naturally asked her how come she'd been out back looking into your sleeping habits, and she naturally changed the subject. But can you blame a man for mulling such words over in his head more than once? The more I studied on it, the less sense it made.

Why would a gal who'd been up in a hayloft with a gent want to spite him to her own husband? You'd think she was a woman scorned, if that didn't sound so impossible. I may be getting old, but I ain't *that* old, and I've seen my woman in her nightgown feeling horny. There's just no way a young stud like you could have turned her down if she'd been up there in the hay with you, right?"

Stringer shrugged and replied, "I'll allow I'd have found such an offer mighty tempting, no offense. What sort of sneakery might she have said she caught me at? I hardly ever jerk off in front of a lady."

Watson smiled despite himself and said, "You'd have hardly had to do that if she was up in that loft with you. She said she went out back to make sure you was comfortable and that you wasn't there. That was when I asked her just how comfortable she meant to make you, traipsing about in her nightgown, and that's when she clammed up. You know what I think really happened?"

Stringer forced himself not to look away as he said, "I'm all ears, since you seem to be all mouth this morning."

Watson protested, "I just got to confide in some damned body, and you're the only man in town I'm sure of. I think she slipped out to play slap-and-tickle with her true lover and that she was afraid you might have spotted her in that white nightgown. So she mean-mouthed you to me afore you could mean-mouth her. Are you sure you didn't spot her slipping off to meet some other man?"

Stringer swore he hadn't seen the treacherous bitch leave the premises. This was the simple truth when one studied on it. So Watson contented himself with another doubtless meaningless threat against his unknown rival. Stringer thought it was hardly possible the poor old gent's woman was only betraying him with one, but it would have been cruel to say so.

He didn't want to hear any more about her, so he muttered an excuse about neglecting Nancy and dropped back to join her and Porter. She shot him a relieved look. Porter said in a too jovial tone, "We were just talking about you. Is it true you can savvy Digger talk?"

"I savvy some Miwok, and all the Great Basin tribes talk much the same and call their lingo Ho. But I don't savvy Yana, the lingo they speak around here. Miss Nancy and me had an English-speaking Indian translating for us. I doubt it could have been him or the Yana we met up with who pegged arrows at us later, though."

Porter went into a familiar speech about Indian treachery, allowing that Diggers were as treacherous as Indians got. Stringer knew better than to argue, and he saw that Nancy, bless her, had neglected to give a full account of their recent adventures. Likely she was sort of shy about them.

To change the subject, Stringer asked the site manager what his future plans were, now that the mine adit was sealed and the smelter out of business. Porter heaved a fatalistic sigh and said, "We quit while we're ahead. As I told you before, this remote operation was marginal at best. Rebuilding the smelter and retimbering the shaft, once we dug it out, would cost thousands. I wired company headquarters on what they left of our telegraph, and they agree it's just not worth it."

Nancy frowned. "Then you mean to simply abandon

the whole town, just as I've gotten to know some Yana?"

Porter grimaced. "Quicksilver was never much of a town to begin with, ma'am. You and your father are welcome to as much of it as we leave behind. It's going to take us a few days, maybe more than a week, to salvage such gear and supplies as we can afford to haul out. Then you and the Indians will have the valley all to yourselves, assuming you and your father want to be so foolish. I don't care how friendly the Indians you met might have been. Some others certainly can't be. I think we must be talking about two different bands, for the ones that hit us last night were hostile indeed."

Stringer said, "Watson just told me outside help is on its way. They ought to be here before you have to leave Miss Gore and her party behind in the valley."

Porter shook his head. "Not now. Once the company authorized us to abandon the site, I felt it my duty to wire both the county and the War Department that the show was over. I don't know about you, but I pay taxes. What sense would it make to have a bunch of soldier boys guarding a ghost town?"

He chuckled bitterly and added, "I guess this time you can say the Indians won. But there's just as much cinnabar down by San Diego, and most of the boys will enjoy the climate a lot more down yonder."

Stringer asked how the moody mine supervisor, Trevor, seemed to be taking the news.

Porter laughed louder and said, "About as one might expect. Old Trevor rates a bonus everytime he exceeds the expected tonnage, and he does that a lot. I swear he has as much gopher as Welsh blood. Right now he's

sore at me because I draw the same salary whether
we're digging or not. But he'll get over it once we shift
the operation south. The company's bought a really rich
lode down yonder, and the local Mexicans are less dis-
gusting to associate with than the Diggers around here."

Watson called back to him, and Porter spurred forward to consult with the nominal leader of the party
about something.

Nancy made a wry face. "I'm glad you broke that
up," she said to Stringer. "He's awfully fresh."

"Oh? Did he make a pass at you, honey?"

"Not yet. But a girl can tell when a man's building
up to one. He was going on and on about how sweet and
willing the Mexican ladies of San Diego act, and he was
allowing that my kind of Gibson Girl, as he called me,
could learn a thing or two from our more natural sisters
in sin. What did he mean by that? You didn't tell him,
did you?"

Stringer shook his head. "You asked me not to. He
was just discussing a favorite subject. There seems to be
a lot of that going on this morning. You've been in
Quicksilver a spell, honey. Have you heard any gossip
about old Watson's young wife?"

"I didn't even know he had a wife. I don't think the
working-class women in town like me well enough to
share such gossip with me. You'd best stop calling me
'honey' in public, lest they gossip about me."

He nodded. "All right, Miss Nancy. What about in
private? Or are you trying to say we won't be meeting in
private anymore?"

She sighed. "I've been thinking about that. You
know I want to. But I don't see how we can in town.

I've enough to explain to Father when he gets back as it is. Can't you think of some place we could meet discreetly?"

He smiled. "I'd better. Watson says he means to gun any rascal he catches with his woman, acting discreet or not."

CHAPTER
NINE

They were all back in Quicksilver by noon. This was
just as well. For Dr. Gore and his two assistants rode in
around one, looking trail-weary and disgusted. As he
joined his daughter and Stringer at the table in front of
their tents, Gore growled, "I swear, I don't know why
we had a revolution and wrote a Constitution just to put
drooling idiots in charge. Nobody at the county seat
seems to know what anthropology is, let alone give a fig
about it. They told me it was up to the town council
here to give us permission or not to excavate. They
seemed to think I was *funny,* damn their rustic brain and
hayseed grins."

"That's all right, Father," Nancy said soothingly.
"We don't have to dig for dead Yana anymore. You'll
never guess what I've been up to while you were away."

Stringer was glad Gore didn't ask for too many details about his daughter's adventures in the hills as she

filled him in on her visit to the Yana, leaving out the naughty parts.

"I have a glossary of the basic words and phrases," she was telling him. "And wait till you see the artifacts we brought back. The Yana are not extinct at all. I think we can get them to work with us. But of course we have to stop digging up their dead, so—"

"Nonsense!" Gore cut in with a scowl. "The bones and artifacts we've excavated so far have to be pre–Gold Rush, if not pre-Columbian. What could a band of miserable modern Diggers know about a lost race that couldn't even be their ancestors?"

"A heap, Doc," Stringer said. "We brought back a basket of the same sort of stuff you've been grubbing out the hard way. If you treat 'em decent, some alive and well Yana may sit still for some hat sizing and maybe even plaster casting. We, ah, took the liberty of assuring them you'd quit digging up their relations. They never asked for any back, so I reckon you get to keep such skulls as you already have. They might come in handy to check against the livelier heads you want to measure."

Gore shook his head, his features set like those of a little kid who just wasn't ready to go to bed yet, damn it. "You have to be mistaken," he insisted. "My whole thesis would be wrong if a superior race of Neolithics turned out to be common Digger Indians."

"The Yana would likely agree they were superior," Stringer replied. "Most Indian nations do. If you'd examine the stuff we brought back instead of arguing about it, you'd see the Yana, ancient or still around, are a cut above your so-called Diggers. They've been living better, here on the west slopes of the Sierra, so they've had more time to spend on their stone working and basket weaving. I'd hardly call a lady who can weave a basket watertight enough to cook in a miserable anything."

Nancy nodded and rose from the table, pleading with her father to at least come look at the fine basket of modern artifacts.

Then young Johnny Conner and the Shasta breed, Uncle Jake, came back from tending to the spent ponies. "Where's that old Paiute woman?" Uncle Jake asked. "The cook fire has gone out, and there's no coffee."

Nancy and Stringer exchanged glances.

Nancy said, "The coffee is here on the table, of course. Granny Bear wasn't here when we arrived an hour or so ago. I assumed she went into town to buy more supplies. But, now that you mention it, she should have come back by now. Wherever could she have gone?"

Johnny Conner said, "No ponies seem to be missing. So I don't see how she could have gone far."

"I do," Uncle Jake said. "Paiute enjoy walking more than the rest of us, even when they're not old, fat, and female. She's been complaining about the way things have been going around here. I think she's superstitious about those skulls in that one tent and decided to go home across the mountains before the snow moons came."

Stringer rose silently to his feet. He hoped he was wrong. So he just said something about asking about the old gal at the general store. Then he strode off fast before anyone could offer to tag along.

• • •

But it wasn't the old Paiute woman they had in a shed behind the town lockup, bedded down in cracked ice from the saloon's ice-making machine. The naked brown remains lay twisted awkwardly in the small crate they'd stuffed with cracked ice and dead gal. The body was more familiar to Stringer than the shot-open face at first. He had to look twice before he was sure it was his old traveling companion, the gal who'd called herself Lola and claimed to be kin to Joe Malliwah. He felt compelled to take off his hat, even though she'd done him dirty in the end. For she was still a woman and, in her time, a mighty sweet little lay.

Clem Watson, who'd led him back to view the remains along with his deputy, Jimbo, cleared his throat and said, "That's mighty respectful of you, considering she was just a wild Indian, if you want my opinion."

Stringer hadn't asked for it. But he said, "You're entitled. She wasn't dressed so wild last time we met. She told me she was a reservation gal and spoke English better than most. I was in fear, as I told you, that you'd nailed the Gores' Indian cook in the dark. I'm glad you didn't. But this one leaves me even more perplexed."

"Try it this way," Jimbo said. "Say she was sort of two-faced. She told white folk one thing and acted another way when she took her duds off with her Indian pals. A Digger spy would sure account for their knowing just where to hit last night, as well as having a naked gal along."

Stringer nodded. He had to, even though he knew he and Joe Malliwah hadn't invited the pretty little horse thief to help them stage a fake Indian attack. The Yana women he'd seen up in the hills hadn't been too modestly dressed, but none of them had run around stark naked, and Lola hadn't even been wearing Yana moccasins when she'd been cut down. He took a quick look at the one bare sole he could see packed in ice. She'd died barefoot, but with little or no dirt ground in. That read two ways: either she'd been stripped after she'd been shot, or she'd been shot indoors, perhaps getting ready for bed, then hauled up the slope to be found later. With all the wild shooting that had been going on, who'd have noticed?

He wasn't ready to confide in anyone before he figured out who might be behind such sneakery. It seemed obvious enough that old Lola, having set him up to be murdered in the hills, had pussyfooted into town to be paid off by the mastermind—and that said mastermind had paid her off this way to silence her forever.

He said he's seen enough, and Jimbo shut the ice chest. As they circled around to the side door of the saloon, Watson wanted to know more about the dead Indian girl. Stringer made up some bullshit about meeting her down near the railroad stop. It was true, up to a point, and seemed to satisfy both lawmen.

Jimbo even opined that the girl might have followed him and been the one who stole his pony. Stringer saw no reason to argue as they went into the saloon to wash the green taste of death from their tongues. As they bellied up to the bar, the barkeep told Watson a stranger had just been looking for him. When the old man asked who, and about what, the barkeep said, "He ought to be back any minute. He just took his pony to the town corral for some water and oats. I told him this would be as good a place to run into you as any."

Halfway down their first beer schooners, as if to

prove the barkeep's good faith, a tall drink of water dressed all in black, save for a big white ten-gallon hat, parted the batwings to ask if the town law had come in yet.

Watson gulped and put a thoughtful hand to his gun grips as he allowed he was the law, and what about it? For the stranger had a commanding stance, a keen stare, and a .45 on each hip.

But he was smiling, however grimly, as he strode toward them as if he owned the place, and Stringer saw that despite his height he was younger than he looked at first.

The young stranger held out a hand instead of a gun. "Howdy. My handle is Tim McCoy, and I ride for the BIA. It's my understanding you've been having Indian problems up here. So they sent me to straighten 'em out."

Watson shook hands with the self-possessed youth. "You mean alone? No offense, we can see you'll be mighty tall when you grow up, Tim. But how good are you at ducking arrows?"

McCoy said soberly, "Good enough. I'm sort of a trouble-shooter for the BIA. I seem to have a way with Indians. In my time I've dealt with Horse-Utes, Navajo, and Apache. It's all in knowing how to talk to them, man to man."

Stringer asked if he'd ever talked to Yana. The young Indian agent looked pained and said, "Not hardly. The Yana are extinct."

Stringer chuckled. "I'd sure like to get some money down on that, if you're a betting man, Tim."

McCoy didn't even seem to be a man who laughed easily. He shook his head. "I never bet on Indian matters. One of the reasons I get along so well with them is that I'm willing to learn. Most Indians hate know-it-alls."

Stringer decided he liked the young cuss, stiff-necked as he seemed. "Well, I'm sure getting saddle sore," he said. "But if you give me time to tell some other folks their cook wasn't shot in the head last night after all, I'd be proud to introduce you to some gents who sure seem to think they're Yana."

Watson said, "Hold on now. You can't take this young boy out into them hills, Stringer. We just this morning saved you and Miss Gore from them savages, damn it."

But before Stringer could argue, the solemn young Indian agent said, "Sure he can, if he's willing. I was sent up here to talk to Indians, and I don't see any here."

As Stringer drained the last of his beer McCoy added stiffly, "It's just as well, too. I don't allow any Indians of mine to drink. I find white drunks hard enough to get along with."

Jimbo asked when and how the local Diggers had become McCoy's personal property.

Stringer said, "We're still working on that." Then he led McCoy outside, saying, "Your own pony won't be up to much mountain climbing after packing you in. We can borrow fresh ones where we're going, unless you'd rather walk."

"That might not be a bad idea, if your mysterious so-called Yana aren't too far. Horses make some Indians nervous, if they don't have any themselves. They're more apt to trust a man on foot not to charge them."

Stringer sighed. "I know. My ass is about as sore as

my feet right now. Let's play it by ear after we bum us a heap of black coffee where we're going."

As they walked the length of town, Stringer filled the Indian agent in on the situation to date and added, "Dr. Gore is no doubt fixing to ask you for a permit to dig up more Yana bones."

McCoy shook his ten-gallon hat. "Not the bones of *my* Indians."

Stringer liked him even more then, even if it was hard to take the pompous big kid as seriously as he seemed to feel he deserved. "Correct me if I'm wrong, Tim. But haven't I seen your face in at least one nickelodeon film? You do present an image to remember, in that big white hat."

McCoy shrugged modestly and admitted, "I picked up a few bucks down in L.A. last summer as a two-bit player in a mighty silly moving picture about the old days out here. They signed me on just to translate for some so-called Apache they'd hired to attack a wagon train in Sioux county. The San Fernando Valley didn't look much like the High Plains, and the Apache turned out to be Mexicans. They asked me to ride into view with news of the attack and said something about a screen test. I never hung about to find out what they meant. The BIA wanted me to lay down the law to some real Apache. I don't see much future in those moving pictures anyhow. I'm sure it's just a fad, like the new safety bikes and side-button skirts the gals are wearing right now."

Stringer nodded. "You're likely right. But you ought to look into it, Tim. There could be more future for you as a moving-picture cowboy than as an Indian agent, at the rate we're running out of Indians."

By this time they'd made it to the Gore camp. Granny Bear was still missing, but Uncle Jake had rebuilt the fire, and there was plenty of coffee.

There was a new face there as well. Another young gent, trying to look older behind a ginger beard, was introduced by Nancy as Professor Nat Robbins, who'd just ridden in. Her father just kept glaring down at the table as if he was suffering an awesome case of bellyache.

Once they'd all been introduced and were sitting down with tin cups poured by Uncle Jake, Robbins seemed to think it was a swell idea to go visit some wild Indians. "Nancy was just showing me her glossary of Yana words. I confess many of them are new to me, albeit they do seem to agree we're saltu and have other loan words from the more familiar Sierra tribes."

"They're Diggers. Just damned Diggers," Dr. Gore spat out on the table. "They're a degraded band of outcasts with a jargon of Shasta, Pomo, and Maidu words."

Nancy insisted, "But, Father, I just told you they have a grammar more complex than Russian."

And their rival, Robbins, had to chime in with, "An archaic Siberian grammar, I'm sure, from the sound of it. Those artifacts you just showed me bespeak folk memories of the Siberian Neolithic too."

Gore growled, "I never showed you anything. It was Nancy's idea to show you those relics she brought down from the hills. I tell you they were never made by any modern Indians. Her Digger friends just dug them up, the same as we have. Everyone knows a band of Diggers was gathering in this valley before the mining company moved in. Who's to say they didn't have such fine flint tools as they uncovered along with their roots and bulbs?"

Tim McCoy, of all people, said, flatly sure of himself, "I don't know anything about Siberia. I've never been there. I do know that no living Indian would touch anything buried with the dead. Not even strange dead. There are cliff dwellings over in the canyon country that are stuffed with pottery, tools, and old mummies. Not even an Apache will touch the stuff, and some pots brought out by our kind are mighty handsome."

Dr. Gore insisted, "That's different. Apache may have a few faults, but they're a proud warrior race. Diggers have no pride. They'll take anything they can get their hands on. The miserable beggers could show me tons of fine artifacts and I'd still know they were just grave robbers."

Stringer muttered, "Takes one to know one, I reckon. We're not going to settle the matter here."

McCoy said he was right and rose imperiously. Robbins rose as well, insisting he was going with them. Nancy wanted to. But they all told her no girls were allowed. Her father said that was the only sensible thing anyone had said for some time, damn it.

It was hot, dusty going through chapparal and tanglewood under an afternoon sun on foot. Young Professor Robbins was getting all pink-faced and kept rubbing his neck with his kerchief. But he was game enough to keep up, and Stringer had to admire the dude. He was having his own time keeping up with Tim McCoy, who insisted on setting the pace and crashed through waist-high sticker-bush as if he thought he was a damned old elephant, even if he was only a moose.

When at last Joe Malliwah let himself be seen on a higher ridge ahead, Stringer started to explain. But the Indian agent said, "I know the rules. Let's see if I can find an impressive boulder to hold court on."

He could, and did. When Joe got tired of waiting for them to come on up and rode down instead, Stringer introduced him to the other white men and explained, "McCoy is the BIA agent we were hoping for, Joe."

The Indian cowboy nodded dubiously and said, "*Bueno.* I'll show you boys close to the band and see if the majapah wants to meet with you."

McCoy said flatly, "I want to meet with him here. Tell him I'll wait no more than halfway to sunset and that I'll be very bitter in my heart if he refuses."

Joe laughed incredulously. "You will, eh? Well, I'll pass your suggestion along, but—"

"It's not a suggestion. It's an order," snapped McCoy, who added, "And wipe that silly smirk off your face while you're at it. MacKail here tells me you served in the Army one time. So did I. As a lieutenant colonel. Do we understand each other, Trooper Malliwah?"

Joe muttered, "Aw, shit." He spun his pony around and rode off fast, not looking back.

Stringer raised an eyebrow. "Were you really a short colonel, Tim?"

McCoy replied with a frosty little smile, "As much a colonel as Buffalo Bill ever was. Indians understand military rank and respect it."

Stringer sighed. "That's what George Armstrong Custer seemed to think. We're talking four handguns between the three of us, Tim. Don't you think you ought to simmer down just a mite?"

McCoy shook his head. "You have to make them feel they're talking to a real man. Real men don't worry about dying, as long as they can die like men."

Nat Robbins smiled weakly and asked, "Could I be excused for the rest of the afternoon, teacher?"

When McCoy failed to smile back, the Indian expert said, "I know a little about getting along with them too. This one's sort of new to me. I generally start by handing out some calico and tobacco."

McCoy said flatly, "I don't. I offer them a square deal, take it or leave it. I treat them as responsible adults, not babies to be pacified with play-pretties."

Stringer chuckled. "I thought the Square Deal was a notion of President Teddy Roosevelt."

McCoy snapped back, "Who do you think I'm working for, the Tsar of All the Russians? The present administration inherited one God-awful tangle of past foolishness, some of it well-meant but most of it designed to line the pockets of both white and red political hacks. The Indian policy of this country is an insult to common sense before you even consider simple justice. We have folks claiming to be one-sixteenth Indian collecting BIA handouts in one part of the country while full-bloods are dying of hunger and TB in other parts. Things can't go on like this. Both a heap of Indians and all the taxpayers are being taken for a hayride."

Nat Robbins smiled. "I take back what I've often said about *everyone* in the BIA, Tim. You'll fail, of course, in the end. But meanwhile, do you mind if I set up shop here until they take your new reservation away from you? I'd like to get a handle on the Yana dialect before they all learn to beg for extra rations in bad English."

McCoy sniffed. "It's a free country, and this part of its reverts to federal open range as soon as that mining company abandons its mineral claim. But there's not going to be any fool reservation here. I mean to enroll this band, whatever they may think they are, as Shasta or Maidu and move them to one reserve or the other. We can't afford a separate Indian Agency for every separate family, can we?"

Stringer frowned. "You were just talking about offering the Yana a square deal, Tim. Is that what you call shoving 'em off their home range to live with strangers who don't even speak the same lingo?"

McCoy nodded. "It's as square a deal as I can give them. No Yana nation exists on the books. I have to put them down as *something,* and as soon as I do, they become wards of the government and off-limits to duck hunters. We've tried bitty tracts set aside as reserves back east. Aside from being a bitch to administer, Indians surrounded by whites on a tiny plot of land tend to be exploited by their neighbors. They're accused of raiding every chicken coop in the neighborhood, and some land-greedy county big shot is always out to get a so-called chief drunk enough to sign away such property as they still have. Until and unless they send some of their kids to law school, Indians are a lot better off on big reserves where their agent can keep an eye on white visitors, and a central trading post, licensed by the BIA, can keep them from being cheated blind."

McCoy saw that Stringer still looked dubious. So he added, "Look, I know it's not a perfect system, and Lord knows the Indians know it's not a perfect system. But it's that or extermination until and unless they learn to cope with our ways. President Roosevelt hopes they will, by the middle of this century. Look how the ex-slaves have learned to make their way in a white man's country."

Stringer said, "I have. Old Teddy always has been sort of an optimistic cuss."

Before they could argue further, Joe Malliwah was back with the old majapah and some other sullen-looking Yana. Joe had made good time and obviously done some convincing talking.

The old majapah got right down to his brag, with Joe translating, and it sounded as if all Indian chiefs had attended the same elocution class, no matter which lingo they spoke. This one wound up by saying this land was his forever, that his eyes were crying blood, and wound up by tearing off his bear-claw necklace and throwing it on the ground as one of his wanasee shot an arrow into the same, between McCoy's boots.

Without rising from his rock throne, the young Indian agent took off his ten-gallon hat, threw that on the ground, then shot it.

As everyone listened in stunned silence, McCoy told Joe, "I want to relay my words exactly. I'll have no bull about a great white father. We're talking about President Theodore Roosevelt, who speaks softly and carries a big stick. Nobody, ever, signed any damned treaty that mentioned running water or growing grass, outside a dime novel. No Yana, ever, signed any kind of treaty with anybody. So they have no legal status at all, nobody even knows how many of them there may be, and nobody, repeat nobody is going to do a thing if an unregistered band is wiped out by anyone they annoy in any way."

He paused while Joe passed that on. The Indians

didn't like it at all, but their ears were still ringing, and they didn't want the dawana saltu shooting his hat anymore. So the majapah just started to argue some more.

McCoy cut him off by drawing his six-gun again with a grim expression as he told Joe, "I don't want to hear idle threats from a handful of dismounted troops. Tell him to forget what he may have heard about past BIA policy. Tell him that this agent also holds a reserve commission in the U.S. Army and that he can forget what he heard about us feeding them in the winter and fighting them in the summer. Tell him I want to be his friend, but that if he wants an enemy he's talking to the right man."

Joe translated, both ways, and the old majapah allowed he'd as soon be friends with such a big mean son of a bitch. They all knew that last remark had been Joe's opinion. But McCoy nodded and said, *"Bueno.* Tell him that for now I want him and his band to stay well away from Quicksilver and their old valley. Tell him I understand the snow moons are coming and that he has my permission to go into winter quarters in these hills for now. Tell him that when the snow melts I intend to give everyone in his band a BIA number and that they have the choice of coming in for their allotments as Shasta or Maidu because I'm such an easygoing gent."

Joe said, "I'll tell 'em. They won't like it."

McCoy said, "Then you'd best explain that I don't have to be so easygoing. I have a cavalry column and a couple of mountain artillery pieces at my beck and call down in Fat Valley. Tell them the soldiers will herd the few survivors any damned place I want them to go, and that the Great Basin Desert is just made for bratty Diggers."

Joe scowled and said, "You can just go to hell, white boy! These are human beings, not infernal livestock, damn your eyes!"

McCoy nodded and said soberly, "I just said I'd treat them as human beings if they'd let me. You're a reservation Indian, if I read your outfit right. Have you been mistreated? Are you held prisoner by your agent, or am I guessing right about you being allowed to work off your reserve as a cowboy?"

Joe grumbled, "It's different for these folk. They ain't as educated as me and my folks."

McCoy replied, "If you and your kin speak Yana, you went through the same educational process. I know you didn't like it. The system stinks. But it's the only one we have, and I see you're still alive and well. I could tell you tales of Indians who insisted on doing things their way. But you've no doubt heard of Wounded Knee and the Washita. So what's it going to be? Wiping out a nation is a lot cheaper than providing for 'em all the way down to their many-times great-grandchildren, you know."

Joe translated. More than once. The Yana pissed and moaned and went into a war dance that inspired both Stringer and Robbins to put thoughtful hands on their gun grips. But in the end Joe said grudgingly, "You win, providing this band gets to leave the reserve during the gathering moons if they can't find all the acorns, bulbs, and toyon berries they need on the reserve. I told 'em my reserve was best for them, even if the infernal agent does insist on calling 'em Shasta."

McCoy said, "I can't speak for the Shasta agent. Once I clear this matter up here, my job will be done. But I don't see why any agent would want to keep well-behaved charges from leaving the reserve for good reason. He let's *you* work off the reserve, doesn't he?"

Before Joe could go into that in Yana, Stringer chimed in with, "The gathering's about shot in that one valley anyway, Joe. A heap of oaks have been cut down, and some of the bulbs are bad eating. A white child died just a spell back, gathering bulbs in this band's old stomping ground."

Joe translated everything. The old majapah seemed as interested in the fate of little Mary-Jo Crocker as anything else. Joe said, "They don't understand that. They had been gathering bulbs, good bulbs, for a long time over there. Even Yana children know what poison bulbs and roots smell like. They always get rid of them. There shouldn't be any death camas in that valley."

Stringer shrugged and said, "Seed must have blown in since they left, then."

But Joe, being Yana himself, didn't have to ask to say, "Hear me, any bulb big enough to eat has to be more than one summer old. Last summer, there were no saltu in that valley. Yana women and children worked those bulb fields over more than once. The saltu child died from eating something else."

McCoy shifted impatiently on his rock and cut in to say it was his understanding they had an agreement and that all would go well if his Yana brothers behaved themselves. Then, when he got no argument, he said, *"Bueno.* I know the gathering has been poor this summer because of those white people. I'm going to send in a mule train of rations and some cough syrup for the kids. I'll want your help in getting it to them, Malliwah."

Joe nodded soberly and replied, "You got it. Just ask

for me by name at my agency, this side of the first snows. Meanwhile, I mean to stay with this band, along with my guns, until I see how well you can get them mining men to behave."

McCoy agreed, and they smoked on it before they split up. On the way back to town afoot, Stringer told McCoy, "That went well. But it just so happens an Army pal of mine told me the Army's not about to march on anyone this late in the season, Tim."

McCoy shrugged. "So what?"

"Just what were you planning on getting all those troops, then, with mountain artillery as well?"

McCoy didn't answer.

Stringer laughed. "I predict a great future for you in motion pictures, once you lose your job as a decent Indian agent, Tim. For nobody but a born actor could have bluffed so brass-balled."

McCoy smiled thinly. "A man works with what they give him to work with, and so far, the BIA has yet to give me all that much. They pay as much as five dollars a day down Hollywood way, too. Ain't that a bitch?"

CHAPTER
TEN

It was almost quitting time down in Quicksilver by the time the three of them trudged in, dusty and thirsty. The coffeepot in front of the Gore tents seemed far enough to walk for now. As Nancy sat them at a table and poured for them, she explained her father was in his tent, feeling poorly.

Nat Robbins raised an eyebrow and asked, "Don't you mean sulking, honey? You were right about those Yana, you know. Some of the loan words they used sounded Shasta or Maidu, and 'saltu,' of course, is pure Ho or Uto-Aztec. Tim here keeps insisting they can't be Yana anymore. He and your dad should get together on a paper. Meanwhile, how do you feel about doing a paper with me on their interesting dialect? They'll still be around, at least until next spring. We could set up shop closer to them, in the hills, and—"

"I know where there's an empty wowi," Nancy cut

in, not looking Stringer's way as she quickly added, "Not that I'm about to spend a winter living in sin, Nat Robbins!"

The young professor grinned. "Just my luck. Maybe I'll have to make an honest woman of you, Nancy. I know your father doesn't approve of me, but you know we'd make a swell team."

Stringer didn't know how *he* felt about that, either. But he knew Nancy would have a red-faced time even talking about it with another man she'd had for breakfast listening. So he got to his feet with an elaborate yawn and said something about seeing how they were coming along with shutting down the mining operation.

He actually headed for the saloon, aboard his now well-rested pony. As he got there and dismounted to rest it some more while he had a beer, a shabby young mining man approached him.

The man coughed nervously and said, "I'd be Lem Crocker, the daddy of that little girl the Diggers dug up. I was wondering, seeing as you just come down from the hills, whether you'd noticed, say, a casket handle in your travels. My wife is mighty upset and—"

"We're not sure your daughter's grave was really opened," Stringer cut in, feeling shitty as he added awkwardly, "It could have been just a dirty trick. Last time I was up yonder I noticed the grave markers were set sort of crooked. There hasn't been any frost yet. It's more likely someone moved 'em."

Crocker blinked uncertainly and asked why anyone would want to do a thing like that.

Stringer said, "It'd be a lot less trouble than really digging all the way down. Someone was out to vex you. They had no real need for a little dead girl, no offense.

Say the pranksters just moved her headstone one notch
over, to where nobody had ever been buried, they'd vex
you just as good without half the trouble. I noticed the
sod was sort of loose down the other way, where there's
no marker at all now. Do you follow my drift?"

Crocker's eyes lit up with hope. "I sure aim to find
out, as soon as I can find me a shovel!"

But Stringer suggested, "Dig at the far end, and quit
when you hit wood where no coffin lies marked. That
way you'll know just as well, and your daughter's remains can rest in peace. For all you'll have to do is shift
each marker one grave over, see?"

Crocker nodded soberly. "I do, and I thank you for
the good thinking. I don't mind saying I wasn't looking
forward to gazing on Mary-Jo's remains again, no matter where they may be. She looked bad enough when we
first put her to rest."

Stringer frowned. "Do tell? I heard she died of
chawing death camas. It's mean stuff, but I've never
heard of it messing anyone up on the *outside*. They just
tend to go to bed after a meal of what they took for fine
onions and never seem to wake up again."

Crocker shook his head. "It wasn't like that with my
daughter. She brung that one bad bulb in with some
others she'd picked. Her mother was watching as Mary-
Jo bit into it, turned red as a beet, and went into convul-
sions, with her poor little lips all blue and burnt. She
died fast, but it wasn't peaceable at all. The doc said
there must have been prussic acid in that bulb. He says
there's prussic acid in bitter almonds and cherry pits as
well. Whatever that bulb was, it must have had a *heap*
of prussic acid in it."

Stringer agreed. They shook on it, and he went into

the saloon as the dead child's father went to look for a shovel.

As he sipped his free beer, Stringer pondered the fate of the unfortunate child. He'd grown up in the same Sierra, eating lots of wild stuff and getting sick on some of it. But, unlike the late Mary-Jo, he'd been tipped off about the really deadly bulbs, roots, and berries before he'd ever managed to kill himself. Stringer considered all the tempting goodies he'd been warned to leave the hell alone, and he simply couldn't come up with any species worse than death camas. He was sure that if there had been anything like a bulb that grew full of prussic acid, someone would have mentioned it to him and the other kids. Most white settlers were careful about stuff a kid could nibble on.

Prussic acid didn't just grow wild in some bulbs, he knew. By its more scientific name it was known as cyanide, and to wind up with burns on her lips that little girl would have had to bite into the nasty stuff at full industrial strength.

He swallowed some beer and asked the barkeep if there was by any chance a photographer's studio in Quicksilver. The barkeep looked blank and asked why he'd ask a dumb question like that.

Half to himself, Stringer said, "Photographers use some cyanide. But you're right. It was a dumb question. I likely need the advice of a botanist instead of a detective. Nobody but a homicidal maniac would have any reason to poison kids with such stuff, even if they had it on hand."

The barkeep said, "If we're talking about Mary-Jo Crocker, she was gathering wild onions or something on an open slope, up above the smelter. We thought about smelter fumes at the time. It didn't work. Mr. Porter allowed some mercury fumes could have settled on the slopes above, and it was his notion to make sure no other kids played there anymore. But mercury poison is way too slow to account for that kid dying from just one bite. You can rub mercury all over you and even swallow some without it harming you. Not a good idea to keep at it, though. Like I said, it's a slow poison."

Stringer agreed he'd heard as much and ordered another beer.

The deputy, Jimbo, came in to order another for himself. He confided, "I'm on duty the minute the sun goes down. May not have this job much longer. They're fixing to leave most of the town behind, supplies and all. The company figures freighting out such stuff as lumber and canned beans won't pay. When was you fixing to haul out, MacKail?"

"Anytime now. That agent, McCoy, seems to have settled your so-called Indian war. I don't write for the society page, so pending wedding announcements are none of my beeswax, and how much serious news could I expect to gather in a ghost town?"

Jimbo nodded sagely, inhaled some suds, and said, "I doubt more than a handful will be wintering over."

Stringer cocked an eyebrow and asked, "Why would even a handful risk a snow-in, Jimbo? I know at least two students of Indian lingo might be staying, further up in the hills. But won't the rest of you be moving on down to San Diego and a new mining camp now?"

Jimbo looked a mite bitterly at his beer as he said, "Those as still have jobs will. I, for one, wasn't on the list that son of a bitching Porter just posted. Seems they don't feel they'll need as big a security force down close to San Diego. Old Clem Watson stuck up for me and the other deputies. But Porter said it wasn't up to him. He's full of shit. I know he never liked me."

Stringer didn't answer. He knew Jimbo could be right or wrong, and it wasn't his fight. He asked why, in that case, Jimbo and the others being left behind didn't go on down to the Sacramento to look for work.

Jimbo answered, "Beans. The rent here will be mighty affordable as well. Nobody hires this late in the fall. I figure to just hole up here and be a well-fed ghost in a ghost town until things pick up next spring."

Stringer allowed that made sense, sort of.

Then Jimbo put his empty beer schooner down, hitched up his gunbelt, and said, "I can see by the sun outside that it's time I made my rounds, lest somebody steal a keg of nails nobody wants anymore."

Stringer didn't argue. He ordered another beer and moved down to the free lunch spread to put away some pickled pig's feet and hard-boiled eggs to keep all that beer from sloshing about an empty stomach and making him talk silly.

He knew it didn't really matter if he got drunk now. But on the other hand there was no point to it with a lonely night on the trail coming on. He wasn't looking forward to riding out in the dark alone. But the story, such as it was, seemed to be winding down, and he didn't want to be in the way when and if old Nancy told her father she was fixing to marry his arch-rival. He still had no answer to those attempts on his life. But now that he'd put the mining operation out of business with his own sly moves, the mastermind was out of business as well, whatever his fool motives might have been.

There was simply nothing left to fight for now, unless you counted arrowheads and Indian skulls.

He put that notion aside as quickly as it arose. Dr. Gore was no doubt eccentric on the subject of lost Indian races, but Stringer knew he hadn't done anything or found anything out that was apt to prove anything either way on the subject.

The dumpy mine supervisor, Trevor, came in to bitch about the mine they wouldn't let him supervise anymore, since it was all caved in. Stringer wasn't about to tell Trevor who'd caved it in. He asked if Trevor was still working for the company. The bitter Welshman said, "I am. But it's all wrong, you see. I was hauling a good tonnage from this mountain up here, and I see no need to start another pit from scratch, look you."

Stringer agreed life was tough and went back to take a leak. When he came back, Trevor had left and Tim McCoy had come in. The Indian agent said, "I was getting tired of listening to those two lovebirds coo. I was planning on riding back to the reserve. How do you feel about keeping me company on the trail?"

"It'll be a lot better than riding alone. We're not about to make it in one night's ride, and I'll be splitting off near the railroad. But by then we'll have told all the jokes we know and gotten sick of one another anyway. You'd best stuff your gut down at the far end before we go, Tim. I ain't up to cooking before I digest the pickled pig's feet I just had, and that can take a spell, you know."

McCoy agreed. They both moved down to demolish the free eats as the barkeep shot them a dirty look. Stringer had eaten all the pig's feet he ever wanted to, and he was peeling a boiled egg when somewhere outside they heard the dulcet tones of rapid gunfire.

As their eyes met, McCoy said flatly, "That was a shoot-out." Stringer didn't argue. They both got rid of their beer steins and dashed out of the saloon as one, staring about in the tricky early-evening light. They saw people running one way and, without having to discuss it, lit out after the crowd, which was heading toward one frame house up the hill.

They joined the crowd gathered about the front gate just as Jimbo came out on the porch, spotted them, and called out, "I reckon this would be your case, Mr. McCoy, seeing as you're the ranking federal man here. I don't seem to be working for nobody no more."

Stringer and the Indian agent bulled their way through to join Jimbo in the doorway. He led them inside, where the first thing they saw was old Clem Watson, spread out dead as a cow pat with a six-gun in one hand and his glazed eyes staring up at the pressed tin ceiling.

"This is Porter's house," Jimbo said. "It get's worse in the other room."

They followed the deputy into the bedroom, where it became more obvious why Jimbo had said he didn't work for anybody anymore.

The site manager, Porter, lay sprawled by the foot of the bed, naked save for the gun he still had in his hand. He'd been shot thrice at close enough range to frizzle the hair on his bare chest.

Watson's wife lay across the bed, without a stitch on and just as dead as the man she'd been in bed with.

Jimbo shifted his chaw and said, "It reads sort of easy to me. But I'd best just see how you boys read it. I don't seem to be a lawman no more, with both the gents I worked for in no position to pay my wages."

McCoy stepped closer to the bed, brushed some hair away from the cheating wife's wildly staring eyes, and said, "Nice-looking gal. You say she was Watson's woman, Jimbo?"

Jimbo nodded.

Stringer said, "She messed around as often as she could get away with it, as I know for a fact. It looks as if this time she didn't get away with it."

McCoy glanced at the open doorway thoughtfully and said, "That's for sure. She took a round right above the eyebrow. It looks as if the old man suspected she was having an affair with Porter at suppertime and burst in on them to ask how come she was in another man's bed instead of at the kitchen stove where she belonged."

Jimbo volunteered, "Watson might have told her he'd be on duty later this evening. I know he talked about that to me a spell back. But then he said he was feeling tired and that I could no doubt handle anything that might come up. He didn't mention anything like *this* coming up, of course."

McCoy nodded. "It must have been a surprise to him as well. Let's say he suspected but wasn't sure. Let's say he came home early to find her gone and came over here to see if he was right or, hell, maybe just to talk to his boss about something."

"Either way works as well," Jimbo said. "The main point is that he caught his woman with another man and did just what any of us would have done. Only old Porter managed to get to his own gun and nail him as well, see?"

Stringer didn't answer. He stepped into the living

room and hunkered down by old Clem's corpse. He couldn't find any bullet holes until he turned the old man over. Then he saw the poor old gent had taken one between the shoulder blades, where his snuff-colored coat had been powder-burned.

As the other two joined Stringer, McCoy opined, "Right. The husband caught them in the act and shot them both. But as he turned to run, the dying lover-boy got off just one shot, and that was just enough."

Stringer got to his feet and asked Jimbo who that left in charge now.

Jimbo started to say nobody. Then he brightened and said, "I guess old Taffy Trevor would be the ranking company man in these parts now. It ain't for me to say. We'd best wire company headquarters and find out."

As he moved for the front door, McCoy said, "You'd best wire the county seat while you're at it. As a federal agent I have power to make arrests on federal property. But Lassen county might not have this township down as federal, as the BIA thinks it is, and in any event, I'm more used to dealing with cases involving Indians."

Jimbo agreed.

Stringer said, "Hold on. Don't you boys feel somebody ought to guard the scene of the crime and make sure it looks the same when someone from the sheriff's department gets here?"

Jimbo said that made sense, too. So, opening the door, he called two company men in and told them, "I want you boys to keep an eye on things here. Don't ask me when, if ever, you'll get a plugged nickel for the chore. Just do it for old time's sake and I'll put in a good word for you with the company. Look around all you want, but don't touch nothing, and don't let nobody else in before I get back to you, hear?"

One of them started to bitch, but Jimbo said, "Now, Roy, we both know the dead bastard in the other room dropped you from the payroll just this morning. Do right by his remains and headquarters just might feel he was hasty in saying your services were a needless expense."

That did it. As Stringer and McCoy followed Jimbo out into the gathering dusk, Stringer asked where the other regular town deputies might be right now.

Jimbo shrugged and said, "Gathering nuts for winter, most likely. Once the company store shuts down, a sack of flour or a can of beans could get hard to come by in this valley."

As the fired deputy continued on toward the remains of the telegraph shed, McCoy said, "I'd best move our ponies from in front of the saloon to the town corral, seing as we're stuck here overnight at least. You coming, MacKail?"

"I'll meet you later at the saloon. Right now I want to gather some bulbs while there's still some twilight left to pick by."

They both asked him how come. So he explained. "That child who died from swallowing poison puzzles me. The Indians say no death camas should be growing in this valley, and I've never met up with any plants in these parts that give off prussic acid."

Neither of them had either, so the three of them split up and Stringer headed upslope at an angle. As he passed the last miner's shack and started to wade through ankle-deep bunch grass he saw no bulb sprouts at all at first. Crocker had told him the child had found some farther up. Stringer could still make out individual blades and pebbles, looking straight down. But more distant features were starting to blur as darkness closed in. A pale blob ahead materialized into the heap of spent cinnabar he'd been told about. They'd sure shoved a heap of the stuff up here, a hundred odd yards above the smaller pile just outside the ruins of the smelter. A mess of wheelbarrow tracks showed how they'd managed. The slope was chewed bare and eroded some by the runoff from the mercury tailings. Some of the grass still there looked sick as hell. Mine tailings tended to leak all sorts of toxic shit when it rained. The low-temperature smelting might not have even gotten all the mercury compounds out of the shattered rock.

He didn't see bulb one on the downward slope, so he circled around to the high side, and while the grass looked a lot healthier here, he didn't spot anything a kid might have felt like picking at first. Then, just as he was about to turn away, Stringer spied what a greenhorn might have taken for onion shoots, and, as he bent over to pull the bulb, a rifle ball plucked at the tail of his denim jacket. So he just kept going down until he lay flat behind the pile of tailings with his own gun out.

Nothing happened for a million years. Then a familiar voice called out, "MacKail! Above and behind you!"

The warning had been shouted by Lem Crocker.

Stringer had no idea who the dark figure skylit farther up the slope might be, but the rascal was aiming a rifle his way. They both fired at the same time.

The rifleman was either a poor shot or perhaps couldn't make his target out against the rock pile in such tricky light. Stringer did better despite its being long range for a handgun. His man threw his rifle end-over-end at the purple sky and fell backwards to just lie there, spread-eagled in the grass.

As Stringer rose and eased up the slope toward him, smoking .38 trained on the still figure, Lem Crocker came running from Stringer's right, a miner's spade in hand. He shouted, "I heard that first shot and hunkered down just in time to see he was circling round behind you, Mr. MacKail. Who was he?"

"I don't know the who or why of it yet, but I owe you, Crocker," Stringer replied.

As the two of them moved on upslope, Crocker said, "I was just on my way down from the burial ground. You was right about them grave markers, and Mary-Jo's momma will be ever so glad to hear them Indians was just funning."

Stringer didn't answer. He knelt down by the man's body and felt at the side of his throat to make sure he was dead, then struck a match.

Crocker said, "Well, I never! It's one of Taffy Trevor's blasters. His name was Swensen, I think."

Stringer shook out the match before it burned his fingers and said, "I may recall him from the time he was getting hell from Trevor about dynamite. It's hard to tell, with his face so clean right now."

"How come he was out to gun you?" Crocker asked.

Stringer could only reply, "Beats the shit out of me. But, like I said, I owe you, Lem. I thought my troubles were about over. I reckon they ain't."

Then he got back to his feet and said, "Come on, I have something else I want to show you."

He led the father of the child who'd died right after nibbling a mysterious bulb back down the slope. Then he pulled the bulb he'd been bending over for just in time and held it up to such light as there was, asking, "Does this look at all like the treat your daughter bit into, Lem?"

Crocker took the bulb, sniffed it, and said, "Exactly like it, damn it to hell. It's easy to see why the poor little thing took it for some sort of wild onion."

Stringer said, "It's camas, not death camas. It tastes sweeter than wild onion, and it's safe to eat, as it was meant to grow. I'd show you, but I'm not sure anything growing this close to mine tailings would be safe to eat."

Crocker stared soberly at the vast pile of chewed-up rock and asked, "You mean my Mary-Jo could have been pizened by this spent ore?"

Stringer shrugged and said, "I don't know. I'm not a chemist. Mercury's a slow poison, and I'd have thought they boiled all of it out of the ore before they threw it away. Arsenic won't work, either. It's found in all sorts of rock, I know. But you have to swallow more than a taste of it, and it doesn't burn your lips like prussic acid."

Crocker asked why, in that case, there couldn't be some low-down prussic acid leaching out of the rock pile. Before Stringer could explain it wasn't a mineral compound, other voices were calling out to them, and they turned to see Jimbo and a modest mob coming up the slope toward them, some packing torches.

Jimbo called out, "What's going on up there? Who's been doing all that shooting, MacKail?"

Stringer called back, "I feel responsible for one shot you may have heard. The other two were fired by the loser, a dynamite hand called Swensen, or so they tell me."

The pudgy mine supervisor, Trevor, pressed forward from the others to demand, "You shot it out with one of my crew, you say? Whatever for, then?"

"I'm still working on that. Crocker here is my witness that Swensen fired first, from ambush. He'll keep as he is for now in this cold night air. We'd best all go on down to the saloon to sort things out in front of the only federal law for a day's ride."

CHAPTER
ELEVEN

Tim McCoy found the latest mystery a poser too. He said he wished a more experienced lawman from the county sheriff's department would show up, damn it.

Stringer said, "I doubt anyone from Susanville has even saddled up, yet. Some ain't as prone to night riding as you and me might be, with gossip of Indians in the air. Jimbo just wired them about the shoot-out at Porter's place as the sun was setting, and they might not know as much as we do about your powwow with the local band. So they might not even start for here before sunrise, and we're talking almost a full day's ride."

McCoy grumbled, "That's what I just said. We have to keep all the evidence as it is until somebody with forensic training can get here."

Stringer pointed out, "The odds on a remote country sheriff having a detective squad are mightly slim, pard. On the other hand, you do have powers of arrest, and

I've done some police blotter reporting in my time. What say you deputize me as your segundo and let's get on with it before the others get away total?"

The mining men crowded into the saloon gasped as one and began to stare thoughtfully at each other.

Jimbo volunteered, "I just can't say every man in town is here right now. But I don't see anyone above the rank of straw boss missing."

Stringer nodded soberly. "I'm glad. Small potatoes don't matter so much and may not know just what's been going on in any case. As most of you know, a mighty sneaky mastermind never wanted me anywhere near this mining operation because he knew a heap more about mining than most of you. But he knew, or thought he knew, I'd covered other mining operations and might know more about the subject than your average newspaperman."

There was an uneasy murmur. Then the stubby Trevor stepped away from the bar with his frock coat hanging open to expose his gun grips as he asked with a scowl, "And then what might you know about hard-rock mining that we don't, look you?"

Stringer left his right boot on the brass rail, his own gun clear, and met Trevor's scowl with a thin smile as he replied in an even tone, "Oh, the mastermind had to know more than me about mining. It's taken me all this time to figure out what he was up to. But, of course, I was sent to cover Indian trouble and might have never paid any attention to less interesting rocks if the slicker hadn't made my life so interesting. That's the trouble with trying to be a slick crook. It can lead a man to making a heap of sneaky moves that just inform the intended victim that some fool game seems to be going on."

Trevor growled, "Suppose you tell us what this game you speak of might be, instead of beating so about the bush, look you."

Stringer said, "I wish you'd stop hovering your gun hand like that, old son. It makes you a nervous man to talk to."

Behind Stringer, Tim McCoy put a thoughtful hand on one of his own .45s and announced, "This is a private conversation between my deputy and Taffy Trevor. I don't want anybody else butting in, and I mean what I say." Then he said, "Go ahead, Stringer. Only get to the point. For any man has the right to draw on another who's accusing him without any proof, as I hope you know."

Stringer asked Trevor if he was fixing to draw. The pudgy Welshman put his gun hand on the bar and demanded to know why on earth he'd want to do a thing like that. So Stringer continued, "Once upon a time there was a cinnabar outcrop nobody knew about but some Indians who only used it for medicine paint. Then a white prospector found it and sold his claim to the big mining company most of you might still be working for. We all know how it was being mined and processed. Only the mastermind thought to test the ore for other metals. He no doubt knew, and was afraid *I* knew, that some mercury ores here in the Sierra contain gold as well as mercury."

That certainly seemed to get everyone's undivided attention. Stringer held up his gun hand for silence, not too far above his gun, and said, "Mercury amalgamates, or mixes, with other metals. Gold is immune to most acids but melts like ice into mercury. The rascal behind all this bullshit knew how to test for gold by using prussic acid, or cyanide. He spilled one hell of a lot of it up around that heap of spent ore. So when a little girl bit into a tasty wild bulb spattered with cyanide, it killed her. But nobody knew why until this evening. Swensen was trying to keep me from gathering ore samples. He—or the sneak he worked for—didn't want it assayed as laced with either cyanide or gold."

In a far corner, Lem Crocker glared at Trevor and reached for his old Patterson conversion.

Tim McCoy drew, threw down on him, and said, "Don't. I know how you feel. But stay out of it."

Trevor was looking green around the gills now as he protested, "You're mad as a loon, look you! Are you accusing me and my smelter crew of boiling mercury out of the ore and casting the tailings aside with higher-temperature gold still in it?"

Stringer said, "Hell, it wasn't hard. You just said gold has a much higher melting point. You must know that's not how you extract gold to begin with. Gold extraction is a cold chemical process. The old-fashioned way involves running pulverized gold ore mixed with water over a bed of mercury. Nothing but the gold sticks to the mercury, and separating them's easy enough. You just said mercury boils off and leaves the gold behind, in this case still in the rock."

"We knew nothing of any gold in that ore, look you!" Trevor almost wailed.

Stringer added, "The newer and best way is to grind the ore as fine as face powder and mix it with cyanide, or prussic acid. The acid only dissolves the gold and leaves the grit solid. You strain the gold-cyanide liquor out and kill the acid with lye so the gold can settle as pure metal. The process is cheap, quiet, and can be done on a small scale in just about any ghost town. The mastermind meant to let the company pay for most of the mining, and, once they abandoned the site, a mere handful of confederates could extract the gold from all that industrial waste they thought they were leaving behind."

Trevor shook his head wildly and protested, "But I am on record as wanting to keep mining, look you! From here the company is sending me down near San Diego to mine more cinnabar! So how could I be this mastermind of your grand Scotch imagination, you see?"

"I never said you were. It was Porter. They never made him overall boss of a mining camp because he was dumb about mining. He kept talking about the gals in San Diego long before you and your blasting crew reached the bottom of the vein up here. I reckon he liked gals to the point of its being injurious to his health. He should have worried more about poor old Watson than me. But Watson's young wife was pretty and more than willing to screw a snake if only someone would hold its head. So we know how *that* turned out, sort of."

Jimbo called out from one side, "Could Watson have been in on that other stuff with the boss, MacKail?"

Stringer replied sadly, "Nope. Porter didn't even tell the poor old gent he was screwing his wife. If Watson had been anything more than a dupe we wouldn't be having this conversation. For a crook with the local law in his hip pocket wouldn't have had to mess around with hired guns and sneaky Indian ladies to stop me. He'd have just had me gunned down here in Quicksilver for spitting on the boardwalk or whatever. Once I made it to the center of his web, the sneaky spider had to play a two-faced game and hope like hell I was as dumb about colloidal gold as the rest of you."

Trevor snapped, "Bite your tongue! It's an experienced hard-rock man I am, and the Taffs I hired myself to work the smelter know a thing or two about mining too, you see!"

Stringer sighed and said, "Shit, I thought I'd just explained that. Everyone here was hired by Porter to begin with. He made sure everyone working under him was simply trained to blast and process any ore they were told to, not to assay it."

Trevor growled, "Thank you very much for calling me a sucker, but since your mastermind is dead and the company has ordered us to abandon the site, I see little profit in further discussion of the matter, look you."

Tim McCoy said, "The man has a point, Stringer. All's well as ends well, and the county law can worry about any loose strings, right?"

"Wrong," said Stringer soberly. "Porter was just the crook who put it together. Watson killed him for another reason entirely. I don't see how a dead boss could have ordered Swenson to make sure I didn't help myself to any ore samples this evening, either."

Jimbo grinned wolfishly and said, "Hot damn! I follows your drift! With Clem Watson dead as well as the boss crook, I'd say that means I get to arrest his segundo, who must have took over the operation, right?"

Stringer nodded but continued to face Trevor as he told the dumpy Welshman, "As senior company official here, you'd have wanted Jimbo to carry on in Watson's place until you packed up and hauled out, right?"

Trevor hesitated, then said, "I would have. Now I'm not at all sure the company will want anyone leaving. Certainly not before we run all the rock we've dug through a more advanced reduction process."

Stringer nodded. "You'll want to appoint some men you really trust as company police, then. We're talking about gold and a two-faced deputy who just shot his own boss in the back."

Jimbo went on grinning vacantly as he went for his gun. But Stringer had been keeping an eye on Jimbo in the mirror behind the bar with just such a move in mind, so he dropped to one knee and spun on it as he whipped his own gun out, and though Jimbo drew faster than anyone who looked so dumb had any right to, it was Stringer who fired first. His first round hit just above the treacherous Jimbo's belt buckle and jackknifed his head down to take the second round in his still grinning mouth.

Stringer's bullet shattered teeth and sent them out the gory exit wound at the base of Jimbo's skull as Tim McCoy shouted, "Stringer! Down!"

Stringer dove forward into the sawdust as Trevor fired—but not, as it turned out, at either Stringer or McCoy. McCoy put a second round in the member of Swensen's blasting crew who'd drawn on Stringer. That one fired the short-barreled .32 he'd had under his overalls into the sawdust between himself and his intended victim before he followed in a stiff-legged fall and never even twitched after he hit with a dull thud, like a tree cut off close to the roots.

By this time one of Trevor's fellow Welshman was blocking the doorway with his own gun out and a stubborn set to his jaw. The older and fatter Trevor shouted something in Welsh and then repeated in English, "The next man who moves a muscle dies like a dog, look you!"

So nobody moved a muscle. Stringer just lay there, smoking gun in one hand, as Trevor snapped, "That's better. Now we want everyone but MacKail and McCoy to slowly unbuckle their gunbelts and step clear of them when they hit the floor, you see."

Nobody argued about that, either. So once he'd disarmed the whole crowd, the new boss of the site began to sort the sheep from the goats with the help of his Welsh pals. Trevor had seen the list made up by the late Porter, and so, as Stringer had hoped, he had a good handle on those who had been "fired" to stay behind with the gold. Most of the men there were honest miners, of course. But Trevor said he felt sure the eight sheepish men his boys had penned in one corner would just love to tell the county sheriff as much as they knew, as soon as the otherwise useless county lawmen arrived.

One of the exposed confederates didn't seem to want to wait that long. He whimpered, "You boys got all the serious ones old Porter recruited, Taffy. I, for one, didn't know half as much as I do now thanks to Stringer. Old Jimbo never told us he shot Watson, and it was him and Swensen as tried to bushwhack Stringer and that gal with arrows."

Trevor cocked an eyebrow at Stringer to ask, "How did you know Jimbo murdered Watson?"

McCoy chimed in with, "That's right. I was there too when the three of us found the three of them dead. Who told you Jimbo was the one who finished off old Watson after he gunned his woman and her sneaky lover?"

Stringer dusted sawdust from his denim as he rose all

the way and commenced to reload, saying, "The sneaky lover told me. Porter had three rounds in his chest, fired point-blank as he rolled off Watson's cheating wife. Did you really think it was possible for a gent in such distress to get to his own gun rig, hanging over a chair across the room? Jimbo was making his rounds and responded to the sound of old Watson's shots. He no doubt found the old man just standing there, gun in hand but heartsick and bewildered. Jimbo simply shot him and had the time to arrange the bodies more artistically by the time you and me got there, see?"

"I do now," McCoy said. "Are you saying you read it that way right off?" Stringer answered with a weary nod, "Suspecting wasn't proving. I figured that once he was free to do as he liked, with nobody left in charge of him, he'd feel free to show his true colors. How was I to know he'd been taught to act two-faced so well?

Old Trevor shot a keen glance Stringer's way and said, "You do know a thing or two yourself about trickery, don't you? Had not you tricked Jimbo into going for that gun, you'd never have been able to prove anything, look you."

Stringer didn't answer. So Trevor put some men to work at cleaning up the mess while Stringer led McCoy outside.

"It looks like we're stuck here until the county can send someone to take our depositions and such," Stringer said. "But, hell, we've got bedrolls on our saddles and it's not quite winter yet."

"I'll be camping a good ways out, then, alone," McCoy answered. "We don't know we got every last one of the gang, and the two of us in one place might make a mighty tempting target."

Stringer shrugged. "The game is up for any we missed. They know they'll never be able to refine the secret gold in those tailings now that it's not a secret anymore. The plan was to extract it sort of private. But now anyone we missed will just have to work for a living like the rest of us."

"I know. But I'm sorry you had to spill the beans about that gold. The last thing my Indians need right now is a gold rush. It was bad enough as it was."

"You won't know they're anybody's Indians unless they're still around come the spring thaw. This valley has been ruined for the Yana in any case, and they might just know some other gathering grounds our kind hasn't managed to fuck up yet."

As they approached the corral and tack shed he added, "There won't be a serious gold rush, with one big mining outfit having claim to all the color for miles." Then they went inside the dark tack shed and groped about in silence for a spell.

Stringer found his Mex saddle in the dark and untied his bedroll. "I'll take the north slope if you'd rather sleep closer to your Indians."

McCoy grumbled, "Bullshit. You want the warm morning sun, and we both know it."

Stringer chuckled sheepishly. "All right, I'll take the shady slope and you can sunbathe, then. I'll see you back in the saloon come morning."

The Indian agent didn't argue.

Stringer hoisted the bedding to his shoulder and headed across town in the dark, jumping the ditch of dirty water along the way. He passed just a few shacks and headed on up the slope. About where the grass began to give way to chaparral he stopped and spread his roll. Then he sat on it to smoke and ponder some.

He had a pretty good feature for his paper, once he strung it together sensible and cut it down to say two columns. What to leave out was always harder to figure than what to put in, for a newspaperman. He knew a lot of his personal part in the saga was unprintable, even if he'd thought it was anyone else's damned business.

He'd built and smoked three cigarettes before he had things about right in his head and undressed to turn in. He'd only been bare under the top blanket a few more minutes when he heard someone creeping through the dry grass.

He frowned thoughtfully and eased a bare arm from under the blanket to quietly haul his six-gun from the rig he'd nested in his overturned hat. As a point of lamp-light from the settlement below winked out and then on again, he had his hitherto invisible target pretty well located. He trained the muzzle of his .38 on it and growled, "That's close enough. I'm not in the market for any magazine subscriptions. So what's left?"

A familiar female voice called back, "Oh, there you are. I thought it might be you, lighting one cigarette after another up there. What on earth are you doing up here, darling?"

As he lowered his gun with a puzzled frown, Stringer told her, "I was planning on spending the night here. Have you and old Nat Robbins asked for your dad's blessings yet?"

She moved closer and dropped to her knees on the edge of his bedroll. She laughed lightly. "Good heavens! Would you want poor Father to suffer a stroke?"

"Not now. I did suspect him of being even crazier on the subject of Indians for a spell. But we just found out who was causing all the trouble around here."

"I know. We just heard. I expected you to return to our camp for some . . . coffee. Is that why you're sulking up here? You thought I was more interested in Professor Robbins?"

Stringer shrugged a bare shoulder and said, "He sure seemed interested in you. I reckon it's a lady's constitutional right to flirt back."

She began to unbutton her blouse as she replied, "I'll have you know that when I shack up with a man it's never a man who spends more time talking about Indians than Father! I'm interested in the subject, to a point. But I'm not about to take it to bed with me! I like Nat. He's interesting to work with. But I fear he'd be an awful bore in bed."

She must not have thought Stringer was, judging from the way she shucked the rest of her duds and climbed in with him as if she'd been invited.

But he didn't feel like evicting the sassy little thing. So as he took her nude body in his naked arms she hugged him back and purred, "Oh, this does feel cozy. Now suppose you tell me all about that showdown in the saloon, and how you ever found out who the mastermind was, you clever soul!"

Stringer kissed her, rolled her on her back, and told her, "Later. Right now I've more important things on my mind."

SONS OF TEXAS

Book one in the exciting new saga
of America's Lone Star state!

TOM EARLY

Texas, 1816. A golden land of
opportunity for anyone who dared
to stake a claim in its destiny...and
its dangers...

Filled with action, adventure,
drama and romance, *Sons of Texas*
is the magnificent epic story of
America in the making...the
people, places, and passions that
made our country great.

Look for each new book in the series!